LORD TEDRIC

The Black Knight of the Iron Sphere

A Star Original

A man whose very origins were shrouded in mystery, he had been a major in the elite Corps of the One Hundred, until he had been accused, and promptly convicted, of plotting to overthrow the regime of Emperor Randow. He had been sentenced to serve a lifetime exile on a vacant, deserted asteroid.

He had escaped, of course, aided by his loyal servant, Ky-shan the Wykzl, another renegade to his own people. The two outcasts had disappeared – no subsequent trace was found of either of them. They were rumored to have fled to the Dynarx sphere.

Tedric smiled faintly . . . Even the young emperor, secure in his palace, was unaware that the entire story of Tedric's treachery was a necessary fabrication devised by the 'traitor' himself.

Other novels in the 'Tedric' series by
E. E. 'Doc' Smith

LORD TEDRIC
LORD TEDRIC: THE SPACE PIRATES

LORD TEDRIC
The Black Knight of the Iron Sphere

E. E. 'Doc' Smith

A STAR BOOK

published by
the Paperback Division of
W. H. ALLEN & Co. Ltd.

A Star Book
Published in 1979
by the Paperback Division of
W. H. Allen & Co. Ltd
A Howard and Wyndham Company
44 Hill Street, London W1X 8LB

Printed in Great Britain by
Hunt Barnard Printing Ltd., Aylesbury, Bucks.

ISBN 0 352 30424 3

CHAPTER 1

Skandos of Prime

On the planet Prime at the edge of the Galaxy, a frail, hunched man dressed in green robes, his face all eyebrows and wrinkles, knelt upon the crest of a hill and stared unblinking at the brilliant spread of stars that occupied the whole of the night-time sky.

The man was Skandos, the histro-physicist; even among his colleagues, the Scientists of Prime, Skandos was recognised as a man of outstanding ability.

This was a time when the Empire of Man, the most sophisticated social achievement in human history, was inexorably entering its final decline, but tonight Skandos was thinking of the past. He was remembering a moment, thousands of years before, when the first primitive spaceship had touched down on Earth's moon after a three-day trip and a mere 240,000 miles.

That, Skandos mused, had been the true beginning of human history. He wondered when would there ever come an end?

He well recalled the intervening years. From the Moon, it had been but a brief journey to the planets and the many habitable satellites of the Solar System. From the outer worlds the first hydrogen-eating ships had begun their slow journeys to the stars, generations passing on board before the final planet-fall.

And then had come the grandest leap of all: the invention of the N-space Drive and the voyage of the *Viola*, three thousand light-years in a mere nine days. With N-space the whole Galaxy had suddenly lain open to the seeking reach of mankind. Bold explorers piloted those first ships but in their wake had come the Scattering, when millions deserted the crowded worlds of the Solar System and went to the stars, to find new homes on a hundred virgin planets.

The Empire of Man developed gradually. Slowly, the political tentacles of Earth reached out to grasp the wayward, wandering children. The first emperors reigned in title only, but real power soon began to evolve in the royal line, until, by the time of the Empress Neva, one lone woman controlled the destinies of twenty thousand billion human beings.

That had been a golden age, Skandos thought. If such a term had any historical valid meaning, then the first few centuries of the Empire of Man, before the Biomen and Scientists had themselves drawn away to carve their own particular roles in the cosmos, when the submen were still regarded as fellow intelligent beings rather than as slaves to be exploited, when new worlds fell almost daily under the allegiance of the emperor, when the Imperial Corps of the One Hundred had preserved peace and law throughout the realm, that had been a truly golden time.

And yet, this constant outward spiral of human ambition had born within it the seeds of its own eventual destruction. Humanity was not alone in the Galaxy. A hundred intelligent species were discovered, studied, discussed, and then swept behind in the wave of Empire. It was inevitable that in time humanity would meet aliens who could not be so easily dominated.

The first of these advanced species was the Dynarx, green slime slugs whose mental processes were totally alien to those of man. The Dynarx ruled a thousand planets of their own, and the first human ships to try and penetrate their boundaries never returned. Others followed, including warships, but the fate of these vessels and their crews was no different. At last, acting from both fear and frustration, the emperor issued an edict declaring the entire sphere of Dynarx influence outside the bounds of human exploration. A portion of the Galaxy was thus lost to human expansion. A relatively tiny portion, true – but it was a beginning, a portent of eventual disaster.

That disaster came with the Wykzl. These creatures, twice human size and covered with blue fur, were more like men than Dynarx. They, too, were building an empire, and for the first time humanity came into intimate contact with an alien species as aggressive and ambitious as itself.

The result was perhaps inevitable: war erupted.

If a golden age had ever truly existed, the thousand-year war between men and Wykzl brought it to an end. Eventually, after millions had died, the imperial fleet met with total defeat and a truce was declared. The war was over and, with it, the age of human expansion.

The century since the end of the war could best be viewed as a period of decadence. Exhausted both spiritually and politically, the Empire of Man declined to a mere shadow of its former glory. Instead of a single emperor, a dozen great families shared power within the realm. Eventually, one of these families, headed by a man named Melor Carey, came to predominate. When the aged Emperor Kane IV died by his own hand, Melor promptly crowned his own son as Matthew I in an attempt to establish a new imperial line.

The reign of Matthew I proved as brief as it was predictable. Rebellion broke out among the frontier stars of the Empire, and the rebel fleet, led by remnants of the elite Corps of the One Hundred and supported by clandestine Wykzl weaponry, vanquished the imperial armada in a great space battle beyond the orbit of Pluto. The old imperial line was thus restored.

To some observers such an event might have seemed an indication of renewed glories, but Skandos was well aware that the Empire of Man had surely passed. The golden age had been the direct result of human innocence, and that quality had long since been consumed in the flames of the Wykzl war.

Despite its peculiar fascinations however, human history remained only a tiny element in the total cosmic picture, and Skandos always strived to glimpse the wholeness, the vast complexity of stars, planets, galaxies, megagalaxies, and universes.

He closed his eyes. His breathing slowed until it was no longer detectable. Forces were at work throughout the universe, and he sought to determine their focal point. He knew the cast of immediate characters: Yod Cartwright, a young man in search of revenge; Lieutenant Jerome of the Corps of the One Hundred; Milton Dass, inventor of the awesome weapon known as the matter-scrambler; Lady Lola Dass, the most beautiful woman in the Galaxy, and Lady Alyc Carey, the most complex. And the prime combatants: the Bioman and pirate Fra Villion, and Lord Tedric of the Marshes. These were the participants, but where was the stage? Ah, here it was. Skandos smiled. Such an insignificant world: Nykzas, a rough frontier planet at the edge of the Empire. Straining, Skandos struggled to observe more clearly.

CHAPTER 2

Yod Cartwright

Squinting through the murky atmosphere of the basement cafe, Yod Cartwright gazed at the blank features of the subman waiter and struggled to think of some appropriate response. 'How about a green *cesma?*' he said tentatively, dimly recalling the name from an old tridee tape and certain it was a spaceman's drink. 'Do you have any of that?'

'Hot or cold?' growled the waiter.

'Ah . . . hot, please.' Yod looked down at the scarred porcelain surface of the tabletop, hoping he had spoken loudly enough to be heard above the din of this crowded room. He would have spoken with more authority except that he was afraid the waiter might take too much notice of him and refuse service. Imperial law prevailed, even on a planet as barbaric as Nykzas, and imperial law strictly forbade the serving of intoxicants to anyone under the age of nineteen; Yod had only just celebrated his seventeenth birthday.

But the waiter, whose hairy arms, pointed ears, and shaggy brow suggested he was descended from a dog or wolf, seemed little concerned with such technicalities. He barely gave Yod a second look. 'You pay in advance,' he said, thrusting out a big hand.

'How . . . how much?' said Yod, fighting the tremor in his voice.

'Give me two solar coins for drink and tip.'

Yod considered asking how that broke down: how much for the drink and how much for the tip. With a sigh he reached into his pocket and fished out a pair of golden coins. The sad truth was that two solars represented exactly one-half of his present fortune. If Fra Villion's representative failed to meet him here tonight as promised, then he was going to be in a great deal of trouble indeed.

The waiter, clutching his bounty, disappeared into the swirling mob, headed in the general direction of the bar. Alone, Yod leaned back in his chair and watched the clientele of this cafe. If there was a more disreputable watering hole in the Empire, he hoped he never had a chance to view it firsthand. The low-ceilinged, brick-walled room was packed with bodies. Every table was occupied, and there were many more people standing in the aisles or by the bar. Submen outnumbered real humans and, from where he was sitting in a relatively undisturbed corner, Yod could count over a dozen true aliens. Some of them belonged to species he couldn't even begin to identify. He did recognise a six-armed Drixian and a squat, purple-skinned, octopoid Zorrazian. Like nearly everyone else in the cafe, both aliens wore heatguns strapped to their bodies. The presence of so much armanent in such a restricted environment only added to the general atmosphere of restrained tension. Yod shifted nervously in his chair and tried to avoid letting his eyes come to rest on any single spot. The fact was, on the planet where he was born and raised aliens were something one read about in books. Six months ago if anyone had told him he'd be sitting in a bar with a dozen of them, he'd have laughed out loud. But this wasn't funny. There was even a giant blue-furred Wykzl seated at a nearby table in the company of a tall blond man of muscular build who was dressed in the tattered remnants of a uniform. The presence of the Wykzl, mankind's sworn enemy, failed to create any particular stir in this place.

A flash of motion, a loud clatter, and the sudden quivering of the table shook Yod from his reverie. Glancing up, he saw that his hot green *cesma* had arrived. It was an alien drink of Sirian origin, if he recalled the tri-dee tape correctly. Before drinking, he searched the tabletop in hopes of discovering some loose change; there wasn't any. He hadn't eaten in nearly twenty hours, and the two solar coins left in his pocket would barely purchase a loaf of stale bread. The distant appendages of his body – fingers, toes, and nose – already felt numb. It might have been hunger but was more likely pure fatigue. He hadn't slept in a day and a half, either.

He raised the mug close to his lips and peered at the steaming green liquid inside. Once, when he had been fifteen, he had stolen some of his father's homemade wine and drunk two full bottles. For more than a day after that he had been sick with fear that he might have poisoned himself – he was that ill. Well, I'm a lot older now, he thought boldly, tipping the mug. He took one cautious sip and blanched. The whole inside of his mouth felt as if it was on fire. Desperately, he swallowed, and the burning spread to his throat and stomach. Gasping, he fought to breathe. His eyes watered. Hot, he had told the waiter – a hot green *cesma*. Well, at least he wouldn't have to worry about getting drunk.

'You've got to gulp it down,' said a voice close to his ear. 'Don't sip, gulp.'

Through watering eyes, Yod looked up at his visitor. She was a young woman. At first he thought she was beautiful but a more careful inspection showed she was merely gorgeous. A trace of subman blood was the one thing preventing her from staking a claim on true human beauty. Her hair and skin were very dark, her eyebrows shaped in a graceful arch that accentuated her slender, high-boned face. She wore a red velvet skirt that circled her hips and was split to reveal the smooth skin of her long legs. Her breasts were bare and she wore a heatgun in a shoulder harness. Something about her appearance made Yod feel distinctly uncomfortable. 'I think it may be a bit warm,' he said, referring to the *cesma*.

'Oh, nonsense. It can never be too warm.' She dropped down in an empty chair beside him. 'Here – watch me.' She wore a strongly scented perfume, and the sweet odour made Yod feel momentarily delirious. Removing the mug from his hands, she raised it to her lips. As Yod watched in amazement, she swallowed a huge gulp of the steaming brew. When she lowered the mug at last, nearly half its contents had been drained. 'Now you try,' she said with a smile; she showed no signs of strain from her ordeal.

Yod wasn't about to be outdone by such a frail young girl. He took the mug, raised it to his lips, and made a courageous effort to swallow. His throat rebelled momentarily, and he was afraid he would vomit, but he finally managed two full, hefty swallows without choking. The top of his skull felt as if it was about to explode from the pressure. 'I see what you mean,' he said, placing the mug gently on the table and wiping his lips dry. 'That stuff isn't at all bad.'

She was laughing at him.

'What's so funny?' he said defensively.

'Your face. It's as red as a cool sun.'

'It's warm in here.'

'I know. But not that warm. Take another drink.' Her eyes, a brilliant shade of green, twinkled with delight.

He shook his head. 'Not now. I have to make it last. I'm supposed to meet someone here and I don't have enough money for two drinks.'

'You're meeting a representative from Fra Villion, right?'

She could have knocked him over with her little finger – he was that surprised. Yod had told no one the reason for his presence here tonight, and he just couldn't believe that this woman was the representative sent by the space pirate. 'Who . . . who are you?' he finally managed to say.

'My name's Juvi.' She extended a hand across the table. 'You must be Yod Cartwright.'

He took her hand in his, pressing gently. She returned his grip with considerable force. 'How did you know that?'

'Just a wild guess. The man I talked to about joining up with Villion said that if I came here I'd find three others waiting. I spotted the first two right away and I figured you had to be number three. He told me your name. You're the only person in this place who could have a funny name like Yod Cartwright.'

'What's so funny about it?'

'It's a farmer's name.'

'Well, I am a farmer. I mean, I used to be.'

'Sure, and now you want to be a space pirate.'

'Yes. Why shouldn't I? What's so absurd about that?' Her amusement was beginning to grate severely. 'I'm quite sure I could handle it better than a girl like you.'

She met his gaze openly. 'What if I told you I'd killed men for saying less than that?'

He couldn't conceal his shock. On Drexon's World, his former home, murder was not a casual matter. 'I – I'd believe you.'

She laughed aloud. 'Then you'd be wrong. But I've thought about it – plenty. My mother left me when I was seven. I never knew my father to speak of. I've had a pretty rough life and I know how to take care of myself. After some of the things I've been through, space pirating ought to be a breeze. See that big guy over there with the Wykzl. Those are the other two I told you about.'

Yod tried to avoid glancing at the nearby table. He had noticed the man and the alien earlier and wondered about them. 'Are you sure? Have you talked to them, too?'

'Not those two, no, but I've seen them around. The man used to be a wheel in the Corps of the One Hundred but they ran him out just after the Great Revolt. It was a political thing, I guess, but he's in disgrace. The reward on his head would be enough to buy a person his own private planet.'

'Then I'm surprised you haven't tried to claim it,' he murmured.

'Normally, I might have thought of it. But not that guy. He scares me. Look at his eyes if you ever get close. They're as cold as a dead star. He would kill somebody as soon as look at them. I just don't want to be that somebody.'

Yod was looking at her closely now. Beneath the painted veneer of her face she seemed almost vulnerable. 'How old are you, anyway?'

'Oh, fourteen or so,' she answered quickly.

'Earth years?' His eyebrows rose in surprise.

'Around that. It's hard to tell. The years are slightly longer here and, besides, nobody ever bothered to tell me exactly when my birthday was.'

She had shocked him sufficiently that he considered taking another sip of the *cesma* to hide his confusion. Fourteen? When he was fourteen, he'd been just a boy. She seemed so damned grown up.

'There isn't time to be a kid on a planet like this,' she said, as if reading his thoughts. 'What about you? What planet are you from?'

'Drexon's World.'

'Never heard of it.' She gave the impression that anything she didn't know about wasn't worth knowing.

'It's in the Rigelian Sphere. Approximately sixty parsecs from here. Drexon's World is the fourth major agricultural planet in the Empire.'

She laughed. 'Farmers!' Reaching past him, she grasped the mug. 'Mind if I grab another swallow? My throat's getting dry.'

He said he didn't mind. The subman who had set up this rendezvous – a hulking creature named Degas covered with scabs and scars – had said nothing to Yod about other applicants. Still, he couldn't doubt Juvi's story. But where was Villion's representative?

'I still don't quite figure it,' she said, lowering the nearly empty mug. 'Why would a guy like you want to be a space pirate?'

This was a question Yod expected to be asked often. He had already rehearsed his answer. 'Excitement, adventure, a real challenge. Look, you laugh at me being a farmer, and I can assure you it's dull. When my father died, I took my inheritance and sold the acreage and came into space. It's taken nearly every coin I possessed to get this far. I visited five planets before Nykzas. On each world I was told I would find Fra Villion someplace else. This time I just hope I've found the right place.'

'Well, he's not here, not personally – nobody knows where he really is. For the past few months, dozens of old spacehands have vanished, and they've all supposedly gone to join up with Villion's band. But you can contact his representatives here. Nykzas is the perfect place for that. There may be worse worlds in the Empire, but if there are then they're so bad everybody's afraid to talk about them. If a corpsman ever tried to sneak in here you'd find a pile of spilled guts in the street the next morning and nobody would do anything except step over it.'

Her colourful descriptive language didn't exactly help ease

the nausea Yod felt building in his stomach. 'All I want is a face-to-face meeting with Villion.'

She smiled at him. 'That may not be easy, even if they let you into the band. I've heard that nobody has ever seen his face.'

'But how can he lead all those pirate raids if nobody ever gets to see him?'

She shrugged. 'Maybe it's just that if you do get to see him, you never go back to tell about it.'

He'd heard this story before, of course, but dismissed it as an unlikely legend. If Juvi's words proved to be true, then it was bothersome news indeed; but what was more immediately disturbing was the approach of the Zorrazian.

Yod had spotted the alien sometime back, its big purple body lumbering across the room, tentacles flapping, and now a dark shadow fell across the table. Yod looked up. There were two immense blue eyes near the top of the egg-shaped mass of the body and a thin slit of a mouth slightly below them.

'Do you want something with us?' Yod asked tentatively.

'Want her to come with me.' The Zorrazian meant Juvi. One tentacle flashed out from its side and caught her firmly by the wrist. 'She has job.'

Juvi glanced up with an expression of unconcern. 'Go away, Dravon. I'm finished with you.'

'No quit me.' The voice was gruff and guttural, like an animal's growl. 'I have signed contract.'

'Then stuff it. I've quit. Now beat it. I want nothing more to do with you.'

'No girl quit Dravon.'

'This one just did,' she said, smirking.

The Zorrazian appeared impervious to argument. The tentacle around Juvi's wrist tightened and a second limb snaked out and caught the nape of her neck. Before she could raise a protest, the Zorrazian had lifted her out of her chair. Only when she was dangling in mid-air did Juvi finally scream.

'Hey, put her down! Cut that out!' Yod took himself by surprise with his own impetuous behaviour.

The Zorrazian had already started to turn away. At the sound of Yod's voice, the alien glanced back. Juvi was pounding her fists against the unyielding mass of its body. 'What you want, boy?'

'I said to put that girl down. She doesn't want to go with you.'

The Zorrazian laughed. At least that was what Yod assumed the grotesque sound must be. 'You shut up, boy, or I make pile of your guts in the street.' Turning again, tentacles waving, the Zorrazian started to cut a path through the now silent cafe.

Yod didn't know what made him act as he next acted. Perhaps it was the fact that everyone and everything in the place was watching him; or perhaps it was simply that, as uncouth as she was, he was getting to like Juvi. In any event, springing to his feet Yod leaped in pursuit of the Zorrazian. The alien was armed with a heatgun and was twice Yod's size but he never even hesitated. The Zorrazian sensed him coming and reached with a free tentacle towards the holster at its side. Yod hurled a fist. It was only when his arm reached the peak of its arc that he realised he hadn't the vaguest idea where to find a vulnerable spot on the alien's anatomy.

So he hit it flat on the top of the head and prayed for help from the Lords of the Universe.

A long, loud, agonised groan escaped from the Zorrazian's slit-like mouth. It's reaching tentacle stopped and hung suspended.

Yod swung his other hand and brought the fist down in the exact same place as his first blow.

It seemed to be a good idea. The Zorrazian never made another sound. Its big body drooped, then fell. The tentacles flopped uselessly. Cast adrift, Juvi landed on her rump. She gazed up at Yod and clapped her hands. 'My farmer hero,' she cried in delight. 'I didn't know you had it in you.'

Yod stepped across the unconscious alien. He was again aware of all the eyes watching him and nearly stumbled in his embarrassment. Reaching down, he helped Juvi to her feet. 'Are you all right?' he asked softly.

'Better than I've been in thirty days.' She kissed his cheek elaborately, then looked him up and down. 'You never told me you farmers were such brutes.'

'Well, your hands get strong when you milk a hundred *bragas* every day for thirteen years.'

She squeezed his bicep in playful awe. 'I'll say.'

Yod looked down at the Zorrazian, wondering what he was supposed to do next. He couldn't help feeling a little anxious. Degas had cautioned him to remain as inconspicuous as possible until he was contacted by Fra Villion's representative. That was no longer possible. He was relieved to notice, however, that almost everyone in the cafe appeared to have lost interest in him. The level of noise was nearly as high as before, and people were stepping across the fallen Zorrazian as if it weren't even there.

'Don't worry about old Dravon,' Juvi told him. 'The way you hit him, he'll be out for another hour.'

'Shouldn't somebody look after him? I mean, what if he dies?'

'A Zorrazian?' You could run one over with a battlecruiser and it'd still get up and walk away.'

Yod was willing to bow to her superior knowledge of Zorrazian physiology. He was about to go back to the table when a new voice caught his attention.

'You hurt my good friend.'

Yod glanced around. A second Zorrazian stood there, bigger, meaner, and uglier than the first. Even worse, it clutched a heatgun in one waving tentacle and the barrel was pointed directly at Yod's heart.

'I kill you,' it said.

Yod backed away. 'I was only trying to help my own friend,' he said. 'He attacked her first.'

'No matter.'

'You want to be fair about this, don't you?'

'No.'

He ran into the wall. With no place else to turn, he held up his hands and waited for the inevitable. Be inconspicuous, Degas had warned him. How inconspicuous would getting killed be considered?

'Zorrazian!' said a voice, as loud as a snapping whip.

Yod turned and stared. It was the tall blond man whom Juvi had pointed out as another applicant for Fra Villion's band, the disgraced corpsman. He had his own heatgun drawn and the barrel was aimed at the advancing Zorrazian. 'Drop your gun and get away from that boy.'

The Zorrazian paused and sneered. 'You asking to die, too, my friend?'

'I'm not asking – I'm telling. Drop that gun.'

'Then you die first.' The Zorrazian turned as if to fire.

It never got a chance. The man's gun bucked once, twice. A flash of flame, a belch of smoke, and then a dreadful odour filled the air. Yod's jaw gaped. A hole as big as a man's head had opened in the middle of the Zorrazian's belly. Inside, the vital organs were clearly visible, black and charred. The Zorrazian gurgled. A stream of blue-purple blood spewed from its lips. It fell, landing on the floor with a dull thud beside the unconscious body of its friend.

The man stepped away from his table. Heatgun still poised, he advanced and kicked the dead Zorrazian solidly in the side. Then he flipped the heatgun in the air. Yod caught it and looked at it; it was old and battered, a much used weapon. 'If you intend to spend time in places like this, keep that handy,' the man said.

'Uh, thanks,' said Yod.

The man reached down and retrieved the heatgun clutched in the dead Zorrazian's tentacle. He hefted it, pleased with his booty, before stuffing the weapon in his holster. He turned, then, and walked back to his table.

Yod felt a tugging at his sleeve. Turning, he found Juvi at his elbow. 'Where have you been?' he asked her.

'Trying to borrow a gun. I guess I wasn't needed.'

'That man saved my life.'

'I know. Mine, too. I saw.'

'We ought to thank him.'

'You'll get ample chance. Our waiter just stopped me. He says, if we want to join Fra Villion's band he's got a cart waiting for us.'

'You mean the waiter was the man all along?'

'The subman. Here, I've got to tell our friend. You stay here.'

Yod made silent agreement. He watched Juvi cross the

room and whisper something to the big blond man, who nodded in return and turned back to converse with his Wykzl companion.

Juvi came back to Yod's side. 'He say's he's ready to go. Hey, did you see the way he drilled the Zorrazian? I knew if any man was mean enough to scare me he had to be pretty damned tough.'

'I wonder who he is,' Yod said, and Juvi looked thoughtfully back at the man.

'Tedric,' she said. 'That's the only name he uses. Just Tedric.'

CHAPTER 3

A Shape in the Night

The mysterious being known as Fra Villion, whose face, it was said, no one had ever glimpsed and lived to describe, was the most notorious brigand in the history of the Empire of Man. Compared with Villion, even a pirate as infamous as Wilson, the renegade robot, seemed no more than a naughty child. At the time of the Great Revolt, against the regime of Emperor Matthew, no one had ever heard of Villion. In the past few months of Earth time, however, he and his crews, plucked from the human and alien flotsam of planets like Nykzas, had ravaged a dozen planets, destroyed a score of spaceliners, and captured twice that many freighters. It wasn't possible to calculate the amount of wealth purloined by Villion and his outlaw band. As far as casualties were concerned, a quite specific figure was available. As of the date of their latest raid, the pirates had accounted for 118,994 men, women, submen, and intelligent aliens dead.

In company with Juvi, Tedric and Wykzl, Yod Cartwright followed the subman waiter through the steam and smoke of the cafe kitchen and out a rear door that led to a narrow alleyway. In contrast to the murky atmosphere of the cafe, the air of the night was cool and sweet. Yod stood motionless for a moment, taking systematic draughts of air deep into his lungs in an attempt to rid his system of any lingering poisons. The waiter pointed to a four-wheeled cart drawn by a large grey-haired *vasp*, an animal similar to a horse, but larger, with long horns and no tail, and said, 'They told me to put you in that.'

Yod peered suspiciously at the cart. It was empty, made from unadorned wood, and quite undistinguished. 'Who told you that?'

'A subman. Vicious little dog. I've seen him around.'

'Does he work for Villion?'

The waiter shrugged. 'I know nothing of Villion.'

'Was his name Degas?'

'He didn't give a name.'

Yod didn't trust this subman. He was still sore that the waiter had overcharged him for the green *cesma* back in the cafe. While that was hardly a crime equivalent to murder and piracy, Yod thought sardonically, it did indicate a tendency to deceive.

Tedric and the Wykzl appeared to entertain fewer doubts. They mounted the cart and after a moment Tedric waved impatiently at Yod. 'Get in the cart. He doesn't know anything.'

'He must know something about Fra Villion,' Yod called back.

'Who me?' The subman laughed with a heartiness that failed to conceal his anxiety. 'A man knowing Fra Villion without a real need is as good as dead. I'd rather know the location of the gates of hell.'

'Then how are we going to get where we're going? If *you* don't know, who does?'

'Why, him of course.' The waiter pointed to the lolling *vasp*. 'He'll know where to take you.'

Yod knew nothing of the animal. Leaning over, Juvi whispered, 'They're very intelligent, like certain birds. They always know their way home.'

'Fra Villion is a sly one,' the waiter was saying. 'The good thing about a *vasp* is that what they know, they can't say.'

Yod still felt hesitant. It was annoying that, having pushed his way to this point his feet were suddenly turning cold. 'All right,' he said, and he found himself forcing the words. 'Let's go.'

Yod climbed aboard the cart and shifted aside to let Juvi find room. The way it worked, he ended up pressed snugly against the Wykzl. The alien turned and peered curiously at him. Unclothed, except for a holster and gun, the Wykzl was covered from neck to feet by a thick coat of neatly preened blue fur. Its face was completely bare, unlined with a flat, pink snout and two round, red eyes. On its forehead, where a man's eyebrows would have been, stood a pair of thin grey tendrils. These served the Wykzl as hearing apparatus, Yod knew, and were supposedly far more sensitive than the human ear.

The Wykzl also stank. The odour hadn't been noticeable inside the cafe but out here it was very clear. The stench was sulphureous and reminded Yod of rotten eggs.

'How does the *vasp* know when to go?' he asked. His voice came out more high pitched than he intended. Nervousness. He still wasn't convinced he was doing the wise thing.

Tedric answered Yod's question with a soft click of his tongue. The *vasp* made a gentle whinnying sound and then started off. The jerk of unexpected acceleration pushed Yod back against the wooden seat.

'I wonder where he's taking us,' he said, as the cart rolled out of the alleyway and into the broad dusty street beyond.

'You mean you don't know?' said Tedric, and there was a sarcastic edge to his voice as he added, with a dry smile, 'The way you've been acting, I assumed you were an old hand at the piracy game.'

Yod frowned. 'If I knew, why would I bother to go through all this? I'd just walk up to the door and knock and go inside.'

'If you tried that,' said Juvi, 'somebody would probably blow off your head before you got a foot inside the door.'

And Tedric said, quietly, 'So why don't we all be quiet and just wait and find out?'

Yod didn't much care for Tedric's attitude. He spoke oddly, too, enunciating each word as if Galactic were not his native tongue. Tilting his head, Yod peered at the sky. The stars looked strange. He had spent too many nights on Drexon's World with his gaze fixed to the sky. The pattern of stars seen from here or anywhere else just didn't seem quite right. It was as if the hand of an unseen deity had stirred up the heavens for mischievous motives of its own. The presence of a pair of yellow moons added to his discomfort. On Drexon's World, there had only been one.

The hooves of the *vasp* beat rhythmically against the stones of the road. Juvi yawned and let her head droop against Yod's shoulder. He tried to edge politely away, but when he did, it only brought him closer to the Wykzl.

The cart turned another corner. Yod had spent a full week in this city, but he already felt thoroughly disorientated. Nykzas was a strange planet. Except for the one city, the entire world was populated by nothing more advanced than a few huge, lumbering, dim-witted reptiles. There were no farms, ranches, or forms of heavy industry. Everything came to the planet through the spaceport, and the city itself originally existed only to feed off that. With the decline of the Empire, trading ships were much scarcer now, and the residents of the city seemed to have adjusted by preying upon one another like cannibals. He wondered if there were any normal people here anywhere, fathers and mothers and children. All he had seen were thieves, conmen, prostitutes, and street urchins. The city was an ugly, alien place, and even Fra Villion's band might seem normal in comparison. If, that is, he ever lived to get that far.

Turning another corner, the cart began to roll gently uphill. Juvi was breathing slowly and steadily and he decided she might well be asleep. The Wykzl continued to peer suspiciously in Yod's direction, while Tedric sat motionless in his seat, his face as cold and hard as solid stone.

Up ahead, there was some sort of commotion. The *vasp* slowed in response. In the street, a trio of young thugs stood in a circle around a single old man. As Yod watched in the dim torchlight cast from a few streetcorner poles, one of the boys reached out and knocked the old man flat on his back. All three of them were upon him at once. Their booted feet lashed out mercilessly. The thump of leather against bone was dull and rhythmic. The old man never made a sound.

Yod jumped to his feet. 'Get away from him!' he yelled.

The boys appeared not to hear him. As the cart rolled past the one-sided battle, the boys went about their relentless work.

Yod turned to leap down into the street and intervene directly.

All at once, there was tremendous pressure on his wrist. He tried to break free but couldn't. Tedric, reaching across the Wykzl, had a firm grip on his arm. 'Sit still,' he said.

'But we can't just – '

'I said sit.' Tedric pulled Yod back to his seat.

'They'll kill that old man.'

'That's his business, not ours. If he can't protect himself, he shouldn't be out in these streets at night.'

'I'm not going to let him die.' The cart was twenty feet beyond the scene now, but there was time to go back.

Tedric released his grip. 'All right, go.' He put one hand on the butt of his heatgun. 'But once you've gone, don't come back. An outlaw band is no place for a man with a bleeding heart.'

While Yod sat indecisively, the entire matter abruptly became academic. While the three boys stood back, the old man came to his feet. He dusted off his pants, put on his hat, and stepped into the shadows. The three boys went with him.

'He's not hurt at all,' Yod said, shaking his head in confusion.

'Of course not.'

'But why . . . what was that all about?'

'Some sort of test,' said Tedric grimly. 'Obvious and very clumsy, certainly, but nearly very effective. Fra Villion must feel the same as I do about bleeding hearts. He wanted to be sure we didn't have one in this cart.'

'Then you really saved my tail just then.' Yod suddenly felt very cold.

'I saved your life. If you'd tried to intervene, those men would have killed you.'

'But why?'

'Because Fra Villion isn't about to let any man come this far, fail and live to talk about it.'

Yod sat back in his seat. Whoever or whatever this man Tedric was, he did seem to understand a lot of what was going on. Up ahead, bright lights were flashing. Yod recognised this part of the town. The spaceport itself was no more than a few blocks away. When he'd first arrived on Nykzas, this was the first place he'd come.

Beneath the steady scarlet glow of a neon sign, the first of the girls stood waiting. It continued to amaze him how young and pretty they looked. There were four of them bunched on the corner. He saw their painted faces and jewelled bodies and looked away, embarrassed by this open display of a commodity he had been taught was too precious to sell.

'Peni, Vel, look. It's me – Juvi.' She was leaning out of the cart, fully awake now, waving her hands.

Two of the girls on the corner stepped forward. One was tall, with pale skin and blonde hair, and the other was short, with black skin and white hair. 'Juvi, where've you been?' said the second.

'Living on my proceeds. I've quit. I'm leaving Nykzas.'

The girl chuckled hollowly. 'Nobody ever leaves here.'

'Well, I am.'

'Then good luck.'

'Good luck to you, too.' Juvi waved, and the two girls went back to their corner. Yod felt his face flush with embarrassment. So that was what she was. No wonder she's seemed harsh to him. He had never in his life expected to meet a girl like that.

The cart rolled on. There were more girls on the next corner and on the one after that. Juvi seemed to know most of them. Occasionally, they saw men, usually palefaced spacemen. All the buildings on this street seemed to be bars and cafes.

'Going to miss your old life?' Yod said harshly, when the cart turned at last on to a dark street.

'A little bit, I suppose,' Juvi said. She had either missed or ignored the bitterness in his voice. Her tone, if anything, was wistful. 'I've been doing it for a hell of a long time.'

'How long is a long time?' He spoke sharply, too sharply. She seemed to become suddenly aware of his slight anger. Looking at him curiously, she said, 'Three years. Since I was eleven.'

'But you were just . . . just a little kid.'

'That's right.' She smiled; on impulse she took his hand. 'Before that, though, there isn't much business and, well, what there is is with clients who are awfully weird.'

Oddly enough, he wasn't as disturbed by what she had said as he thought he should have been. With anyone else, the whole story might have seemed sordid, but with Juvi it seemed natural – necessary. He didn't think she was really a bad person. After all, how could he judge her life? Just because he had had every advantage she lacked was no reason for him to feel superior. 'I'm sorry,' he finally told her.

'Sorry for what?' she said, letting go of his hand.

Ignoring her question he said, 'You *have* quit, haven't you?'

'I'm retired.'

The cart had left the more crowded precincts of the city and was now ascending a particularly steep hillside by way of a winding road. The houses up here were much larger and more ornate than the stone buildings below, and several were completely hidden from view by thick shrubbery and tall trees. The road was wide but poorly maintained, filled with bumps and ruts that made the cart buck and heave.

'I've never been to this part of the city before,' Yod said.

'A lot of people haven't,' said Juvi. 'Hardly anyone lives up here, it's so isolated and exposed. They're mostly rich recluses who live here.'

'And rich pirates, like Fra Villion.'

She shrugged, yawning again. 'If he's really up here.' She laid her head against Yod's shoulder, a deliberate gesture this time. 'Wake me if we ever arrive.'

Yod could only envy her calm. As far as he was concerned, every additional inch the cart rolled on increased the tension welling up in his gut. Striving to ignore the gentle whisper of her breath so close to him, Yod turned to Tedric in hopes of finding some common ground for conversation. 'You said you thought those men in the street were there just to trick us. Would Fra Villion really go that far to test us?'

'He'd be a fool if he didn't. Every weak link in a band of outlaws puts you that much closer to prison or death.'

'You talk as if you know all about it.'

Tedric shrugged. His gaze remained fixed to the road ahead. It was clear he did not intend to talk about himself.

'But you did save my life back in the cafe,' Yod went on, refusing to give up and fall silent. 'I do owe you a debt of gratitude for that.'

'Why? I didn't have much choice.'

'The Zorrazian wasn't angry at you. It was mad at me.'

'I doubt seriously that it was mad at anyone.'

'I knocked out its friend. It was ready to kill me for that.'

'I've never known a Zorrazian to have a friend, its own kind or any other. They're brave but they have no loyalty. I doubt that the first one cared much about the girl, either. Women like her are no rarity on Nykzas.'

'Do you mean that was a test, too?'

'More than likely. A Zorrazian will do anything for money and their lives mean little to them. Fra Villion wanted to see how you'd stand up under stress.'

'Then I must have passed. That's why the waiter took us to the cart.'

Tedric nodded silently.

'That still doesn't explain why you helped.'

'Because it couldn't hurt. I suspect Villion knows who I am, but I wanted to be sure he didn't forget.'

'You must know plenty about him, too.'

'Not that much. When they asked me to join the band, I didn't see any reason to refuse.'

'They asked you?'

'The subman did, Degas. They say he speaks for Villion.'

'Didn't you belong to the Corps of the One Hundred at one time?'

'It's possible.'

'Well, didn't you – ?' Yod stopped short. Tedric, turning in his seat, fixed him with a fierce stare that seemed to say that this wasn't a wise subject to pursue. 'I'm sorry. I didn't mean to pry.'

Tedric's voice was friendlier than before. 'Curiosity is very human. It's nothing to be sorry about.'

'You don't seem especially inquisitive yourself.'

'Don't I? Look there.' He pointed ahead. 'I think we've arrived.'

Yod recognised the house they were approaching. It stood at the peak of a high hill and was clearly visible from the city below. He understood that the huge mansion had once belonged to the imperial governor during those centuries when the visible arms of the Empire had stretched even this far. 'This can't be the place we're going, can it?'

'Why not?'

'It's so . . . so huge.'

'Maybe Fra Villion likes to keep his men in style.'

The *vasp* quickly confirmed Tedric's judgement. The road ended shortly beyond the big house, and the beast turned aside, drawing the cart through a pair of iron gates. Electric illumination poured from the lower windows of the house, and the broad front porch was also well lighted. Standing near the door was the figure of a large man.

As the cart drew to a halt in the thick grass in front of the porch, the figure moved towards them. It wasn't a man; it was a robot. The frozen features of the face and the stiff motions of the knees gave that away almost at once.

The robot stopped beside the cart and bowed awkwardly. Yod had seen few such creatures before. He knew they were incredibly expensive and usually limited to technical duty aboard interstellar ships.

'I welcome you to the house of Lady Lola and Milton Dass,' said the robot, in a voice as harmonious as good music. 'The master is presently engaged on a project and sends his greetings. He has directed me to show you to your rooms.'

Yod glanced at Tedric, whose expression gave no indication that he thought anything was out of order. Yod was curious, however. He had come here to enlist in Fra Villion's outlaw band, so who was this Milton Dass? Some sort of lieutenant? He felt he had a hundred questions, but Tedric's silence kept him quiet.

'If you'll come inside with me, please,' the robot said.

With a resigned shrug, Yod stepped onto the grass and helped Juvi from her seat. Here in this strange yard dominated by the vast bulk of the house and the bizarre form of the robot, he felt like a character in a dream. With Tedric, Juvi, and the Wykzl, he mounted the steps, crossed the porch, and entered the house. In the first room, numerous works of art hung on every wall and corner. A kinetic sculpture, close to the door, showed two huge beasts locked in mortal combat. As Yod watched, one of the beasts, a four-legged monstrosity with spikes on its tail, killed the other, a giant cat with fangs as long as its skull. Then, just as quickly as the end had come, the dead animal regained its feet and the battle commenced again.

'Does it please you?' the robot asked.

Yod tore his eyes away from the oddly hypnotic scene. 'I – yes. But it is very weird.'

'The work of my mistress,' the robot said. 'Some have called Lady Lola the most beautiful woman in the Galaxy, but others have praised her as its most profound artist. Beasts such as these roam the plains of Nykzas and yet few have ever seen them. This statue is an attempt by Lady Lola to capture the brutal fact of their existence.'

'I think it's scary,' Juvi said. She looked uncomfortable as she watched the kinetic display. 'It's frightening.'

'Are life and death considered frightening?'

Yod felt totally bewildered. This robot talked as if it were in love with this Lady Lola. That wasn't possible, was it?

As Yod climbed the stairs behind the robot, he listened to the echo of his footsteps. Was the house empty except for the robot and, presumably somewhere, Milton Dass and Lady Lola? All Yod knew was that this place was not what he had expected. He had anticipated a dirty, one-room hut filled with foul-smelling submen. That was the tridee version of an outlaw band. It certainly wasn't this – a huge mansion filled with works of art.

The second floor of the house was as deserted as the first. A broad corridor stretched both ways from the staircase, and there were blank white doors set at regular intervals. The robot turned to the right and opened the first door that it came to. 'Tedric, you will take this room, please.'

'I would like Ky-shan to stay in the same room.'

The robot bowed. 'As you wish.'

Curious, Yod peered past the robot at the room beyond. It was big and comfortable, with a large bed, thick carpet, two chairs, and a bookcase. There were two paintings on the walls, stark desolate landscapes. Lady Lola again, he assumed.

The robot led Yod and Juvi to adjoining rooms across the corridor from Tedric.

Alone at last, Yod stretched out on the bed and struggled to arrange his confused thoughts. A heavy silence spread around him, and he wondered for a moment if the room might be soundproof, but when he went to the door and peered out, the silence was just as profound as ever.

He wasn't tired anymore. His head on a soft feather pillow he stared at the smooth white ceiling above. He thought about Fra Villion, and the Zorrazian in the bar. He thought about this strange girl Juvi, and he thought about this even stranger man Tedric. He thought about his home on Drexon's World, and he thought about the family he had once loved.

Still restless, he stood, crossing to the window and drawing back the shade. His room overlooked the rear of the house, where a flat expanse of well-trimmed lawn sloped downhill, punctuated here and there by clusters of sentry-like evergreen trees and batches of bright nocturnal flowers. It was a peaceful view from here, with the soft light of the twin moons merging with the starker illumination spilling from the house. As Yod watched, he suddenly noticed a figure. Someone was taking a walk down there.

He knew it wasn't the robot. This figure was completely different. It was huge, nearly as tall as the Wykzl and twice as broad. Dressed all in black, with a cape spilling past its shoulders, the shape – was it a man – paced rapidly back and forth, head thrown back, face not quite visible, arms moving swiftly at its sides. Who could it be? Yod wondered. Hilton Dass, the apparent owner of this house, or someone else entirely? Then something very odd happened. The figure suddenly appeared to divide so that there were two identical shapes moving across the lawn. It was a fantastic event, one that Yod found impossible to accept as anything more than illusion; but no matter how furiously he blinked his eyes or shook his head, the figures refused to merge again. Am I going out of my mind? he wondered vaguely. For a time he thought sure he was merely dreaming.

Then, between one glance and the next, the lawn was empty again.

Distantly, he thought he heard the closing of a door. When he turned and looked, Juvi stood behind him.

He jumped, startled like a child shaken from a deep sleep.

'Hey, what's wrong with you?' she said, hesitating.

He pointed to the window. 'I saw . . . I thought I saw . . .'

'Saw what?' She walked across the room and looked out into the night. 'I don't see anything except a lot of trees.'

'There was a man – two men. I think they were men.'

'Who?'

'I don't . . . ' And suddenly, he did know. 'It was Fra Villion.'

She laughed. 'You're crazy.'

'It had to be him.'

'How do you know? Was he wearing a big nametag around his neck?'

'I know because . . . ' He started to tell her about how the man had separated into twin images of himself. But he stopped. His words sounded absurd even in the privacy of his own mind. 'Who else could it be?'

'Well, Milton Dass, for one. He owns this house, and I hear he's crazy. It could be a gardener. A prowler. It could be almost anyone.'

'It was Fra Villion,' he repeated firmly.

'And the other guy?'

'What?'

'You said there were two men.'

'No. No, only one.'

She stared at him curiously. 'Boy, you really have had a long day.'

He tried to laugh in response. He knew what he had seen and there was no use trying to share it with someone who hadn't. 'What are you doing here anyway?'

'I thought I'd sleep with you.'

'With me?'

She shrugged. 'Sure, why not? I don't think Tedric's in the mood and, besides, he scares me. The Wykzl isn't my type, either.'

'But I'm not . . . '

'Not what?' Dropping on the edge of the bed, she began to remove what few clothes she wore.

'Not your husband,' he said.

'So?'

'On Drexon's World, sleeping with someone before marriage is punishable by death.'

'How come?'

It was something he had never considered before. Her nakedness disturbed him. It shouldn't have mattered – her garments had left little enough to reveal – but somehow it did. 'I don't know. It's always been that way.'

'And you're a virgin?'

'Well, no.'

'Then what's the problem now?'

'I just can't. I'm too nervous.'

'Don't you like me?'

'Sure, I do.'

'Then don't worry. You'll be okay.' She extinguished the light. It was funny. He hadn't even realised that the switch was located by the bed.

As he went towards her, he glanced over her shoulder at the window. He saw nothing.

CHAPTER 4

Lord Tedric

As soon as he heard the footsteps of the robot disappearing down the staircase, Tedric reached beneath his shirt and removed a small cylindrical masking-scanner fastened to his skin. Pressing down on one end with his thumb, he pointed the device slowly around the room. A soft, steady humming emanated from its interior. After completing a full three hundred and sixty degree circuit of the room, Tedric lifted his thumb and the humming ceased. He refastened the device to his chest.

'It should be safe to talk now,' he told his companion, Ky-shan the Wykzl. 'If anyone is trying to listen in, he'll only pick up static. I'll keep the device emitting from now on, so we should remain safe.'

'But won't the silence itself arouse suspicion, Tedric?' Ky-shan had lived among men so long that he spoke Galactic with only a hint of an accent.

'I'm not sure it matters. They know I belonged to the Corps and shouldn't be surprised to discover I ran off with a few of their gadgets. Only a fool would broadcast his private conversation when he doesn't have to. I doubt that Villion wants to let a fool into his band.'

'If you have nothing to hide, why should you care?'

'Everyone has something to hide. This way, I keep them guessing about what it is.' Tedric lay on the big soft bed and rested his head in the palms of his hands. The nape of his neck was beginning to throb and he sensed the beginning of a blinding headache. He shut his eyes and slowed and deepened his breathing. Ky-shan studied him with a look of concern. Tedric fought to clear his mind. 'Besides, we don't really know what we're up against here. None of the intelligence reports concerning Nykzas mentioned Dass or his wife being involved.'

'Do you know them?'

'Not personally, no, but I've heard of them both. Lola Dass is exactly as the robot described. She's beautiful and brilliant. I've also heard she's as mean and unscrupulous as a Drixian at moulting time. Milton Dass is a good bit older. He's a scientist, a physicist, probably the most distinguished alive in the Empire today. We studied his work when I was a cadet at the Academy.'

'And he lives here?'

'He has for years. His father was in the imperial service, an ambassador and governor. That's probably where Dass obtained this house.'

'But what's his connection with Fra Villion?'

'I haven't the slightest idea.' Tedric rubbed his neck. The pain was beginning to ebb.

'And these other two. The girl and the young man. What do you make of them?'

'Trouble, I would guess. Even if we were alone, this wouldn't be easy, and those two are apt to get in the way. I haven't the slightest idea why Villion sent them here. I'm a big catch for the band but they're just kids. Usually, recruits are just taken to the spaceport and whisked away.'

'But they're not typical pirates, either.'

'No. Juvi I can figure out. She's young and bored and too intelligent for the life she's lived. But Yod Cartwright puzzles me. I can't figure him out.'

'He has to have some reason for being here.'

'That's what worries me. Villion's ships have raided a number of backwater worlds. In the bar, when he was talking to Juvi, did Cartwright mention the name of his homeworld?'

The hearing apparatus of a Wykzl was superior to that of a human. Ky-shan was capable of listening to several conversations simultaneously – and at long distances. 'I believe he said it was Drexon's World.'

Tedric frowned. 'That was one of them. I remember. Villion raided the major cities and burned a lot of the outlying precincts.'

'Then you think it may be revenge that has brought Cartwright here? He doesn't stand a chance.'

'I'm afraid he may be bitter enough to try anyway.'

'What can we do?'

'Very little. Villion undoubtedly knows as much as we do. He remembers Drexon's World, and he can add two and two. If he let Cartwright come this far, he must have some reason.'

'To kill him?'

'If that's all he wanted, he could have done it long before now.'

Ky-shan sat slumped in one of the chairs. 'Perhaps I will rest. There is little room for action now.' His slim, elongated body dwarfed the frame of the chair, but he showed no discomfort.

'Go ahead,' said Tedric.

'We will converse once more in the dawn.' Ky-shan shut his eyes. In a few moments he was fast asleep, his breath coming in regular noisy gasps.

Tedric gazed at the alien envious of the creature's ability to relax. He had beaten the headache but he still hung a long way from restful sleep. When was the last time he had experienced the pleasure of genuine inner peace? Not since long before his trial, forced exile, and subsequent escape – that much was for certain. In this universe? More likely in that other one, that dimly remembered place from which the Scientists had wrenched him.

Tedric shut his eyes and rubbed his temples. If he couldn't sleep, at least he could attempt to relax. Tedric the traitor, he thought – that's me. If a more notorious criminal existed in the Galaxy, then it could only be Fra Villion himself. Tedric pretended not to care. Let people think what they wanted to think. As long as he knew the truth himself, what else could matter? But Lady Alyc Carey didn't know. He was convinced she must guess the truth. Alyc would never accept the idea that Tedric had deliberately turned against his own sworn loyalties. Would she? What about his own confession? Would she believe that? Alyc was back home on Milrod Eleven in the Quixmass Sector. He wished he could go there now and ask her. Well, what do you think? Am I a traitor or not? Which do you believe? Me – or the words I was forced to say?

A man whose very origins were shrouded in mystery, he had been a major in the elite Corps of the One Hundred until he had been accused, and promptly convicted, of plotting to overthrow the regime of Emperor Randow. He had been sentenced to serve a lifetime exile on a vacant, deserted asteroid.

He had escaped, of course. Aided by his loyal servant, Ky-shan the Wykzl, another renegade to his own people. The two outcasts disappeared – no subsequent trace was found of either of them. They were rumoured to have fled to the Dynarx sphere.

Tedric smiled faintly. It must have made quite a story for the newstapes of Old Earth. Besides himself and Ky-shan, only one other person knew the truth: his old friend, Phillip Nolan, Commander of the Corps. Even the young emperor, secure in his palace, was unaware that the entire story of Tedric's treachery was a necessary fabrication devised by the 'traitor' himself.

It was because of the red clouds. The first of these had appeared within the realm of the Wykzl some twenty common years before. The clouds were constantly-expanding objects capable of swallowing up anything that stood before them including inhabited star systems. In the years since that first cloud had been discovered, more than two dozen had followed, ranging in diameter from a hundred light years to as small as a few thousand kilometres. What had happened to those worlds engulfed by the clouds? There was no way of finding out, for once a planet disappeared inside the mass of a cloud nothing was ever heard of it again, and no instrument had yet been devised capable of penetrating the veil. Many Wykzl believed that the clouds were more than mere astronomical phenomena. Some thought that they were sentient creatures acting in a conscious way. This was not proven, however. What was known for certain was that when a cloud approached a planetary system the inhabitants began to experience horrible waking dreams that drove them mad long before the cloud actually arrived to devour their world.

For the Wykzl, the danger presented by the clouds, had

recently become dramatically immediate. Two very large clouds had materialised near the centre of their realm, and within a hundred years, at their present rate of expansion they would swallow ninety per cent of the Wykzl population. The only strategy as yet employed to evade this menace was that of mass evacuation; with their available resources this was proving to be an enormous task.

Besides the clouds within the Wykzl realm, a number had also been located within those star systems inhabited by the Biomen; just because relations between the Biomen and the Empire had long ago been severed, no reliable information concerning the extent of this menace was available.

Until recently only the Empire of Man and the Dynarx, of the four major species in the Galaxy had been spared from attack by the clouds.

Tedric himself had been among the first human beings to set eyes upon a red cloud.

Mo-leete, a Wykzl who had assisted the rebel forces during the Great Revolt against Emperor Matthew Carey, had taken him to the spot. The cloud was not a particularly large one, and its rate of expansion was relatively slow. Tucked away in a remote, uninhabited corner of the Empire, it offered little immediate danger to human life and imperial civilisation.

Still, it did exist, and was the first cloud to be found in the Empire, it was certainly a fore-warning of the invasion to come. Tedric was deeply troubled by its presence – and quite justifiably so.

As soon as Emperor Randow was securely seated upon the imperial throne, Tedric sought permission from his commander, Phillip Nolan, to revisit the site of the red cloud and examine it more closely. He went, accompanied by Ky-shan, his servant, and by Lady Carey, the younger sister of the dethroned emperor. Alyc had long since deserted her usurping brother. She had stood close to Tedric's side during the violent battle in space which had effectively brought an end to the rebellion and the brief reign of Matthew Carey.

Tedric had spent several weeks orbiting the expanding mass of the cloud, but he discovered nothing useful: the cloud refused to divulge its mysteries so casually. In the end he had returned to Earth and recommended to Phillip Nolan that a constant watch be kept upon the cloud.

The watch was assigned – and almost immediately rewarded. A lone ship of non-imperial design was observed leaving the cloud. At first this seemed impossible. The Wykzl were quite adamant that nothing, once it entered a red cloud, could ever emerge again. But the ship on watch had not only observed but also photographed the alien craft as it left the intruder. Tedric studied the photographs and saw no choice but to accept what they represented as the truth.

An attempt was made to trace the path of the alien vessel, but since it had entered N-space soon after its exit from the cloud, this was not possible. Then, a few months later, a deserted ship of unknown origin was discovered in a remote area of the frontier planet, Dimetros. A squadron of corpsmen searched through the inhabited lands of the world, but none of the colonists, or military installations, reported having seen a thing.

The question was left open; filed but not forgotten.

In less than a year came the first attack by a band of pirates under the leadership of someone known as Fra Villion; the attack occurred within four parsecs of Dimetros. The second attack was seven parsecs distant and the third, twelve.

Coincidence?

Possibly. But from the moment he had heard the pirate's name, Tedric had sensed that Fra Villion and the ship that had emerged from the red cloud were very intimately connected. Fra Villion had been a passenger aboard that ship. Tedric had suffered from similar feelings several times before, and he had long since learned not to discount them. He had no evidence – no hard facts – but he was certain he was correct.

Phillip Nolan, who knew Tedric very well, was inclined to agree. As the months passed, and the number and severity of Fra Villion's raiding missions increased, Nolan grew more and more concerned.

It was Tedric who suggested that the only way to find out the truth about Fra Villion was to send an infiltrator into his band.

CHAPTER

Fra Villion

When Tedric opened the door to
incessant knocking from without,
eyes. A man stood in the hallwa
twitching at his sides. The ma
ing people Tedric had seen in

'You're Tedric?' said th
as a boy's.

'I am.'

'Great. I'm Dass – Milto
you.'

'Villion? Here?'

'Sure. Where else did you expect to find
into the room. As soon as he saw Ky-shan aslee
his whole demeanour changed. He seemed even mo
bright-eyed, wondrous boy. 'Is that a Wykzl? A real Wy

'That's Ky-shan,' said Tedric.

'I've got to talk to him! I'll wake him up.'

Tedric hastened to intercept Dass before he could disturb the Wykzl. Few creatures of any sort appreciate being roused suddenly from a sound sleep, and Ky-shan was no exception. Tedric steered Dass towards a safe corner of the room. 'I'll take care of that in a moment.'

'But I've got to talk to him. Don't you understand? I've never seen a Wykzl before. It's amazing, simply amazing.'

It was all Tedric could do to keep from laughing at Dass's childlike excitement. The man's appearance did not help much, either. He was short, thin, frail, with a face as wrinkled as an ageing prune. His hair was an orange-grey thatch as thick and stiff as wires.

Nolan concurred, but what
ever was picked would have
but also several hundred of
outlaws in the Empire.

Tedric suggested himself.
Nolan laughed and pointed
known after the role he had
Revolt. Someone in the p
someones – would recognise hi
be his death.

It was then that Tedric suggested the su
supposed treachery. At first Nolan refused poin
his friend through such a terrible ordeal, but Tedric
there was no other way and at last Nolan agreed.
And that was how he came to be here now, in this house,
waiting for morning to break.

Ky-shan continued his peaceful slumber. Outside, the sun did at last appear to be creeping past the horizon's edge. Standing, Tedric stretched his legs and tested his muscles. Then he went to the window and looked out.

From here, at the peak of the hill, the city lay spread out beneath him, brown and dull in the grey light of dawn. The only indication of life came from the bright circle of the spaceport, where a single silver ship was just now rising into the air. As the slim cylinder of the ship ascended slowly the roar of the primitive rocket engines reached Tedric clearly in spite of the distance involved. Higher and higher the ship climbed and tilting his head, he continued to watch as it broke through the lowest clouds and plunged towards the blackness of unseen space. For a long time, even after the ship itself had become too faint to see, Tedric stared in wonder at the tiny flicker of flame still visible through the thick mass of clouds. Then, finally, there was nothing.

Leaning back, Tedric shook his head. He was a man who had piloted many ships at N-space velocities. He had travelled twice around a sun in less time than it had taken this one ship to disappear from view. Despite this, he did not think he had ever seen a sight quite so awesome as that chugging, heaving, straining rocketship, struggling to break free from the gravity

, but a different Earth,
forces of raw magic still held
back there. Skandos had once offered
had refused. It was behind him, passed,
man of this universe. The collective human
that rocketship was part of him. He would never
never glimpse that old home again.
Tedric turned towards the bed. His head ached, and he
suddenly eager to rest again.
But at that moment someone knocked at the door.

...ally awoke in response to the voices in ... surprised and bewildered, too. He stood up, ... eyes with the tips of his fingers.

'This is Milton Dass,' Tedric explained. 'He says he's come to take us to meet Fra Villion.'

'Villion?' said Ky-shan. 'Here?'

'Where else did you expect to find him?' said Tedric, with a wry smile.

Dass was circling Ky-shan, his eyes wide in his head, his tongue constantly clicking. At last, pausing only a few inches in front of the tall alien, he thrust out a hand. 'I understand, during the war, your species made a habit of eating human babies.'

Ky-shan stared. He didn't seem to know whether he ought to shake Dass's hand or bite it. 'I don't believe my people ever – '

'Not true?' said Dass. He dropped his hand suddenly and turned away. 'A pity, actually.' He never explained why he felt that way. Reaching Tedric, he opened his left fist and revealed what appeared to be a shiny brass ball. 'What do you think of this?' he asked.

Tedric shook his head uncertainly, but Ky-shan, who had crossed to join them, was less diplomatic. 'It's nothing but an ordinary brass ball.'

Dass laughed. 'So it might seem. But watch what happens when I rub it.' He shut his fist, wriggled the knuckles, then opened his hand again. A burst of bright light exploded from his palm. Tedric fell back, shielding his face, and Ky-shan cried out in surprise.

Dass's high-pitched, childlike laughter filled the room. 'Look,' he cried. 'See what I've made for you.'

Tedric looked around him. The room had been transformed. From wall to wall, floor to ceiling, it was filled with several thousand brightly sparkling, tightly packed, miniature points of light. They were stars, he realised, tiny stars.

'It's nothing but a hologram,' Ky-shan said; he was clearly unimpressed.

'Oh, that, sure,' said Dass, 'but much more, too. Can't you tell? It's a map – it's the Empire of Man. See here?' Dass turned quickly and marched to one corner of the room. When he passed, the stars in his path winked out of existence. Once he was gone, they sparkled to life again. 'Here is the sun of Nykzas way over here.' He indicated one tiny white pinpoint. 'And over there by you, Tedric, is the sun of Earth. It's all complete – with a magnifying lens you can even see the planets – and perfectly done to scale. Of course, in this limited space, our bodies get in the way, but the idea is to hurl the map out in front of you and then study the portions you want at your ease.'

'But where did it come from?' Ky-shan said, turning his head as he stared at the detail. 'How did you make it?'

'Have you forgotten this?' Dass held up the brass ball between thumb and forefinger. 'It all came out of this.'

'Impossible,' said Ky-shan flatly. 'A hologram requires the use of – '

'The impossible happens to be my business,' Dass said glibly. 'If I couldn't do that, how could I claim to be what I am – a genius?'

'I don't believe you.'

'So? I don't believe you either – about the babies. Now watch this.' Tucking the brass ball inside his fist once more, Dass again moved his knuckles. In an instant, the vista of stars had vanished. Tedric thought he might have seen a brief flash of motion, the stars rushing towards the fist, but he could not be sure. Dass grinned at Ky-shan. 'Want to tell me that was impossible, too?'

Ky-shan snorted angrily. 'I am merely a common soldier. The scientists of my race – '

' – are no smarter than the average scientists of mine,' Dass completed. He tapped his forehead. 'In other words, without much imagination. The map was a little invention I rushed out one summer to keep myself amused. I suppose it has some practical value in terms of space navigation, but I'll leave that for others to worry about. Here, my Wykzl friend, call it a present.'

He tossed the brass ball casually across the room, and Ky-shan caught it. Cautiously, the Wykzl tucked the ball beneath the broad belt of his holster.

'Now come along, you two,' said Dass, with sudden impatience. 'We really can't keep Fra Villion waiting much longer.'

As Dass turned to open the door, Tedric glanced at Ky-shan and smiled. Ky-shan indicated his own amusement. Only the obvious practical value of Dass's invention prevented them from laughing aloud. It was obvious that Milton Dass was exactly what he claimed to be – a genius – but there was a strong suggestion of madness in his behaviour.

Yod and Juvi were waiting in the corridor. From the way they glanced at Dass, Tedric guessed that both of them had already been similarly treated.

'I wish I could serve breakfast now,' Dass said, as he led the way downstairs, 'but I suppose this appointment is more important. I've tried to make cooking into a science. When my wife was here, I once cooked a five-course dinner for the both of us in less than three minutes.'

'Where is your wife?' Juvi asked.

The question seemed innocuous enough, but Dass's reaction was almost violent. His jaw dropped, his spine sagged, and his voice choked. 'Fra Villion will tell you that when you talk to him.'

They reached the foot of the stairs, passed through the room with the sculptures and paintings, and entered another. It was a large bare room with a wooden floor. 'If you'll sit down and wait,' Dass said, 'I imagine Fra Villion will be with you in a moment.'

Turning, Dass left the room through another door. His step was slow, like a man lost in thought.

Juvi whistled softly. 'Who, in the name of the Lords of the Universe, is he?'

Tedric shook his head. 'He's a brilliant scientist. I suppose he has a right to be odd.'

'And the way he acted when I asked about his wife. I think he's under some kind of strain. He seemed nervous to me. I know men. He was talking and moving all the time to keep from thinking.'

Tedric shrugged. 'Whatever, he seems harmless enough.'

'Then I guess he didn't show you what he showed Yod and me. We were still asleep when he banged on the door. He came racing in and went through this crazy routine and ended up asking me what I thought of this thing in his hand.'

'Was it a brass ball?' asked Ky-shan.

She shook her head, clearly surprised that the Wykzl had addressed her directly. Tedric knew that though Ky-shan was shy around strangers, he was beginning to feel more at ease with Juvi and Yod. 'A chunk of plastic. It looked like something broken off a kid's toy. He told us it could kill and I laughed in his face. Then he went over to the window, opened it, and threw the thing out. There was no sound at all. When I looked out, there was a hole in the back yard big enough to fit a small lake.'

Tedric grew thoughtful. Among the more puzzling aspects of Fra Villion's career was his ability to wreak incredible amounts of damage with such a small force of men and ships. Milton Dass's soundless bomb might go a long way towards explaining the apparent anomaly.

The big house was silent now. Dass had disappeared and there was still no sign of Fra Villion. Of the four of them, Yod Cartwright seemed to be the most nervous. He sat by himself, chewing his lip and absently stroking the butt of the heatgun Tedric had given him. Tedric recalled his suspicions of the previous night and slid furtively closer to the boy. If Fra Villion really was about to appear among them, he did not intend to let Yod do anything that might end up harming them all. Surely Fra Villion was not a fool. He would never be so reckless as to expose himself to those whose loyalty he could not guarantee.

A heavy thumping, squeaking noise resounded from the rear of the house and grew steadily in volume. Eventually, Milton Dass reappeared, pushing a heavy iron box supported on four wheels. The box was nearly as tall as Dass himself.

He stopped in the centre of the room and wiped the sweat from his face. 'That's real work,' he said.

'What is it?' asked Juvi, indicating the box.

Dass grinned and tried to sound casual in spite of his obvious fatigue. 'Oh, just something Fra Villion wanted me to bring.'

He swivelled his head as if in surprise. 'He should have been here by now.'

'We haven't seen – ' Juvi began. She broke off suddenly, her face twisting in surprise.

Tedric could see it, too. A large shape was materialising in one corner of the room. As he stared, the shape took form. It was a humanoid creature, nearly five metres high. A coat of thick black fur covered the body from neck to toes, but the face, except for patches of smooth black skin on each cheek, was a tumult of rainbow colours – blue streaks, red and yellow splashes. At first Tedric assumed that this beast must belong to some bizarre subman breed, but he quickly changed his mind. This thing was in no way human; he could sense that. It was alien.

'Fra Villion,' said Dass stiffly, and with difficulty he managed to execute a quick bow. 'I am honoured to see you again.' There was an edge to his voice, painfully obvious sarcasm.

Tedric fought against his own sense of wonder. The apparition was simply another hologram, he told himself; nothing more. If Dass could pack a few thousand stars inside the shell of a brass ball, then this enormous beast could easily have materialised from inside the core of a concealed pinhead.

But Dass wasn't acting as though Villion was anything less than real, and Tedric doubted that subterfuge was numbered among the inventor's talents.

And there was another significant difference: the star map was not alive; this beast was.

A deep musical voice emanated from the huge shape. 'I am Fra Villion, and I am pleased to greet each of you.' The head turned slowly upon the wide shoulders. 'Tedric. Ky-shan. Juvi. Yod Cartwright. I recognise and welcome you all.'

Tedric decided to forget being bewildered. He had to assume this thing was actually Fra Villion and act accordingly. He had to play his assigned role. 'Hold on,' he said, coming to his feet. 'I didn't come here just to talk to a hologram. I want to see Villion – the real Villion.'

The beast chuckled softly. Smiling, it revealed a pair of sharp yellow fangs.

'I mean what I say,' Tedric persisted. 'I didn't come all the way up here to have tricks played on me by some tinkerer like Dass.'

'And I didn't either,' said Yod, though with less assertiveness. He stood beside Tedric.

'Then come forward and touch me,' said Villion, addressing Tedric. 'I don't mind the intimacy. Once you have done that, your own senses will verify my reality.'

Tedric saw no way to refuse. Besides, he was curious. Stepping forward, he held out a hand and touched the beast's middle. The fur was cold and stiff, reminding Tedric of icicles, but it was real enough.

He stepped away.

'Well?' said Villion, in a voice that boomed. 'Do we talk or do we not?'

'I don't know,' Tedric said truthfully.

'Am I real enough to merit your attention?'

Tedric finally nodded. 'Go ahead and talk.' He glanced at Yod, who had also touched the beast. The boy was trembling. Juvi, on the other hand, seemed more awestricken than terrified, while Ky-shan maintained his usual calm demeanour. Tedric backed away and sat on the floor again. 'I'm listening.'

'Excellent,' said Villion, with a hint of sarcasm. 'I have come to you today for only two purposes: I wish to notify you of your acceptance into my band, and I wish to provide you with an initial set of instructions.'

'We thank you for that, Fra Villion,' Tedric said, with his own hint of sarcasm.

Villion went on without pause. 'A ship is presently awaiting you at the spaceport. It is an advanced craft of my own design, fully capable of travelling at N-space velocities. Tedric, you will command. The others will serve as your crew. I make the assumption that a man of your character would prefer to associate with people who are not confirmed pirates.'

Tedric shrugged. 'Isn't that more or less what I am these days?'

Was that a hint of amusement in Villion's face, Tedric wondered. If it was, it might mean that his masquerade was succeeding – Villion had accepted him as a renegade.

'Your ship has been programmed to travel to a certain point

in the Damabi Sector. Since this happens to be where my headquarters are located, I hope you'll forgive me for not revealing the exact co-ordinates at this time.'

Tedric managed to conceal his surprise – and delight. The red cloud was located in the Damabi Sector. More and more he was convinced that there had to be some connection.

'On your way, I have one small assignment to divert your energies. There is a planet close to your route that happens to possess native resources capable of providing a considerable obstacle to my present activities. For that reason, you will pause on your course long enough to destroy this one world.'

Tedric controlled his shock and then managed to laugh. He hoped his voice sounded cynical enough to fool Villion. 'Destroying a planet is not quite as easy as you make it sound. One ship can't do it – not one little tug.'

'Thanks to Milton Dass, it can. Milton, explain to Tedric the capability of your latest invention.'

Dass looked both excited and fearful. 'It's really quite simple. I call it matter-scrambler. Direct the ray, push a button, and any solid matter in its path will be broken down into its component molecules and then scattered into space.

'That's impossible,' Tedric said, but he was far from convinced. 'Dass had already provided sufficient examples of his ability to suggest he *could* perform the impossible.

'I regret the difficulty of providing you with a demonstration,' Villion said. 'The matter-scrambler presently exists only in a crude form and is not very selective. Milton has cautioned me that to test it here might well result in the accidental destruction of Nykzas itself, which would be a most unfortunate occurrence, especially for those, like yourself, who will be present at the time.'

'Then you haven't been able to test the weapon? You can't be sure that it works?'

'The only definite way to test such a device is to use it. Once you've left Milrod Eleven, then we'll know.'

'Milrod Eleven?' Tedric repeated, shocked and stunned. Milrod Eleven was the home planet of the Carey family. It was where Lady Alyc Carey lived. He sensed that Villion had devised a perfect method for discovering his true loyalties, and this realisation gave him an empty feeling deep in the pit of his stomach.

'Milrod Eleven is the planet I referred to earlier, the one I have chosen to destroy. Do you object, Tedric?'

He had to decide how much of the truth he could safely conceal. More than likely, Villion was at least partially aware of his relations with Alyc Carey. He said, more calmly, 'I know someone who lives there.'

'The planet is almost totally uninhabited.'

'She's a good friend of mine.'

Villion's face remained expressionless. 'You may refuse the mission if you wish, and leave now. As long as you reveal nothing you have learned today, I will make no effort to stop you.'

Tedric considered Villion's offer, even though he doubted its sincerity. If he left now, his only chance to infiltrate Villion's band, the end result of many months of difficult preparation, would be ended. He peered closely at the looming shape, hoping to discover somehow a clue to the beast's true intentions. 'All right, I'll stay,' he said at last.

'And you'll allow Milton to test his device against Milrod Eleven?'

'Yes.'

'Despite the presence there of your . . . friend?'

'Yes.' The word stuck in his throat briefly.

'And what about the rest of you?' said Villion. 'Any compunctions concerning what I've asked? Milrod Eleven is a nearly empty world. There are no more than two or three residents there. Juvi, what about you? Are you willing to serve?'

She didn't seem eager, either. 'I asked for this. I won't back out now.'

'And you, Milton?'

Dass had taken a seat on the edge of his black box. He was frowning with peculiar intensity. 'You know I'm going. We made a deal, remember?'

'And the shedding of human life does not disturb you?'

Dass started to make a heated reply, then shut his mouth. His head drooped. He was as sombre now as he had been ebullient before. Tedric guessed that Villion was taunting poor Dass about something. He wished he knew what. 'Leave me alone,' Dass said in a cracked voice.

Villion shifted his attention again. 'And you, Yod Cartwright? Are you with – ?'

Like a tightly drawn spring suddenly set free, Yod bounded to his feet. He drew his heatgun and screamed. 'You murderer! You bastard!' Before anyone could move an inch, he fired off two clean bolts. Tedric leaped for him. Yod twisted away and fired two more shots.

The crackling bolts of high energy flashed across the room. Juvi dropped to the floor, and Milton Dass flopped beside her. Spinning around, Tedric caught Yod around the waist and pulled him down. He got a grip on the boy's wrist and twisted. The heatgun shot free of his grasp. Yod was kicking and yelling. 'Let me go. He killed them. Don't you understand? It was cold blooded murder.'

Tedric let him go. Standing quickly, he retrieved the heatgun and shoved it in his belt. Only then did he glance across the room. Fra Villion stood unharmed. Behind him, four huge streaks showed in the wall. 'I'm afraid, Yod, that you can't harm me now,' he said.

Yod was sitting up. His body shook with rage and frustration. 'I had to try it. I couldn't come this far and do nothing.'

Tedric understood the situation. This wasn't the real Fra Villion they were seeing here. In spite of its apparent reality, the figure was merely an image of some sort. Despite Yod's worst efforts, Villion remained unharmed.

'My question remains unanswered,' Villion said. 'I need to know whether I have a complete crew.'

Yod looked up, astonishment combining with his anger now. 'You're still asking me to come up with the others?'

'I haven't a great many alternatives. If you won't come, the mission will be delayed.'

'Then I am coming,' Yod said, the fury back in his voice. 'But if I do, I won't stop. I'll find you, and I'll try to kill you again. I swear I will.'

Villion faced them all, ignoring Yod's threats. 'The *vasp* and cart will carry you to the spaceport. The ship's registration is in order, so you may leave immediately. Until then, I look forward eagerly to seeing all of you again.' He turned his head towards Yod, and a thin smile broke through his features. 'Most of you, at least.'

Then he was gone. The shape vanished as suddenly and mysteriously as when it had first appeared.

For a moment, too stunned by what they had witnessed, no one said a word. It was Milton Dass who finally broke the silence. 'I'll need some help with this,' he said, standing and indicating the black box.

'What is it?' Tedric said.

'My matter-scrambler. The parts are in here. I suppose I'll have to fit it in the ship's guns before we leave Nykzas.'

'And it works?'

Dass nodded flatly. 'I know it will. You see, I did the original theoretical work years ago. No one was interested. Until Fra Villion. He came to me, told me he'd seen my work, and asked me to develop a practical device.'

'And you agreed?'

'I had little choice.'

'But – ' Tedric stopped himself. There was little point in exploring any of this now. 'Yod, Juvi, give Dass a hand with his box. Push it outside and put it in the cart. We'll be leaving soon.'

The three of them went away. When Tedric and Ky-shan were alone, the Wykzl came up to him. 'That creature, Tedric, it was not real.'

'No, it was some kind of projection. I wish I knew how he did it.'

'I think I know. When I was a child on my own world, I saw something similar. It is done with the mind, a mental projection. It is said that they may cross hundreds of light-years in such a fashion.'

'They?'

'The Biomen *vemplar*, the black knights.'

'Are you saying that Villion is a Bioman?'

'I am nearly positive.'

'He certainly didn't look human to me.'

'The Biomen are a separate race.'

'So I've heard.' Tedric shook his head. No Bioman had been seen in the Empire of Man for centuries. What would one of them be doing here now? What connection could it have with the red clouds? He started for the door. 'Maybe we'd better go out and help the others,' he said.

CHAPTER 6

Dethroned Emperor

This won't do,' said Matthew Carey, the former reigning potentate of the Empire of Man, glaring at the breakfast plate of processed ham and fried hen's eggs that sat on the table before him. 'It's barely even cooked.'

'I'm sure the kitchen followed your directions explicitly, sir,' said the subman who had brought the meal. The creature was some sort of sullen dog with a sneer of curlish contempt upon its thin black lips.

'How dare you use that tone to me!' cried Carey, pushing back his chair and springing to his feet.

'I merely told the truth, sir. Your breakfast is no different today from yesterday.'

'Are you calling me a liar, idiot?' he screamed, shaking with rage.

'Not at all, sir,' said the subman softly.

'Then take this meal away and bring me something fit for an emperor.'

'But you're not the emperor anymore, sir.'

Carey could not believe his ears. Was this thing – this stupid animal – daring to provoke him openly? Reaching out in his fury, he grabbed hold of the underside of the table and jerked up. The table tilted and rocked, and the plate of ham and eggs slid neatly off. Striking the floor on edge, the plate split in half. Egg yoke spread across the thin, frayed carpet in a yellow pool. Carey dropped the table, breathing heavily from his anger. 'Now pick that up,' he told the subman. 'Clean up this mess and get out of my sight.

The subman shook his head. 'I can't do that, sir. I'm a waiter, not a cleaner. I'll have to fetch someone else.'

'I ordered *you* to do it!' cried Carey.

'Well, I can't, sir. Imperial proclamation. We submen can't be treated as slaves anymore. We have jobs – the same as anyone else.'

Carey didn't think he could bear it. His life, these past few months, had consisted of one humiliation after another. Racing around the corner of the table, he reached for the shards of broken plate, but by the time he had retrieved the largest piece and flung it, the subman was already safely gone. The plate struck the back of the door, broke into a dozen smaller pieces, and dropped uselessly to the floor. Carey stepped in the pool of egg yoke. His bare foot nearly slipped out from under him and he strained his knee trying not to fall.

In frustration, Carey sat down on the floor. He put his head in his hands and wished he could cry. It was so unfair – so wrong. Hadn't the black beast itself guaranteed that he would reign for a lifetime? From that ultimate power, reduced to this: the object of a subman's scorn. *You're not the emperor,* he had said. True – how true. The black beast had promised, and the black beast had lied.

Carey looked up suddenly, sensing that he was being watched; something was happening in the room. Over by the door a shape was materialising, a huge dark form. He rubbed his eyes, unable to accept what they told him. It couldn't possibly be – (a shrill, almost hysterical giggle escaped his lips) – the black beast had returned! For the first time since the defeat of the imperial fleet in space by the band of renegades led by his old enemy Phillip Nolan, the beast was daring to appear before him. For a time, he had even doubted its real existence. It might have been a dream, a fantasy induced by the rapid flow of events at the time. Yet here it was again. He knew it well.

As the shape slowly spread into the figure of the black beast, Carey came to his feet. Even then, standing, he felt overwhelmed by the awesome size of the thing. It took up the whole of the room from floor to ceiling, a good five metres in height. Its body was covered with a thick pelt of black fur, but the face, totally bare, gleamed in a rainbow whirl of painted flesh. Carey staggered back, his anger tinged by genuine fear.

'So you have come to doubt my reality, Matthew Carey,' said the beast, in a deep melodic voice. It was as if the thing could read Carey's inner thoughts.

'You deceived me,' he said, battling to keep bitterness from his voice. He didn't want to shout. The cleaning servant might appear at any time and he didn't want a rumour to get started that he talked to himself. They already thought him a fool. He didn't want to be regarded as a madman, too.

'I deceive no one,' said the beast. 'Those I represent miscalculated the seriousness of the Wykzl threat.'

Carey was convinced the beast was lying. 'A miscalculation? Is that how you describe it? I was guaranteed my throne for life. Instead, I have this – this *box* room.'

'And yet you are alive.'

'Who do I have to thank for that? Prince Randow – Emperor Randow! I convinced him that I posed no immediate threat to his reign. He stuck me here to make sure.'

'He could have executed you.'

'So? Do you call this living? Sometimes I wish I really was dead.'

The beast laughed, a booming chuckle. 'Where there is life, Matthew, there must be hope.'

'Well, not here,' he said sullenly. 'Thanks to you, thanks to those you represent, whoever and whatever they are, I have nothing.'

'I bring glad tidings.'

Carey watched the beast coldly, but inside he felt a burst of renewed hope so powerful that he could taste it on his tongue. 'What tidings?'

'Those I represent have decided that you will rule again.'

Carey laughed. 'Do you expect me to believe that? Is it what you told my father? Lies, lies, and more lies until finally you deserted him and he died alone. Who are you talking to now? Is it Randow? Nolan? I wouldn't put it past you. I trusted you – I ignored my own father – and I was ruined.'

'Your father ignored the advice offered by those I represent. He was cautioned that the time was not ripe for your rule. But he went ahead – and he failed.'

'You never bothered to tell me any of that. According to

you, it was just fine that I was emperor.'

'Those who I represent deal only with what is, not with what might have been. When your father went ahead and established you on the throne, it became an established fact within the shifting fabric of the cosmos. You are our only friend in the imperial sphere, Matthew Carey. If we defeat our ancient enemies, then you, too, will emerge triumphant.'

He laughed hollowly, taking in the chaos of the room with a broad sweep of his arms. 'If I'm your friend, then I'd hate to see your enemies.'

'Be silent.' The beast spoke softly, but its words were like a command. It had first appeared to Carey during the brief period when he had ruled the Empire. It had advised and counselled him, proclaiming that it had served his father in a similar capacity for many years. Carey didn't know what the beast was or where it came from. He knew it was strange and powerful and claimed to represent unseen creatures even stranger and more powerful. With the beast on his side, he had felt for a time that he could not possibly fail. 'I wish to know about the man, Tedric, and his alleged treachery to the realm.'

Tedric. The name was very familiar to Carey. Even before, the black beast had always been asking about Tedric. Carey knew the man only vaguely. He was a brute, without family or last name. Big, strong, powerful, but not invincible. Carey had once defeated Tedric soundly in a fist-boxing match. He could remember his triumph keenly. 'I know very little of the matter. Neither Nolan nor Randow is apt to confide in me. Tedric emerged from the rebellion as quite a hero. I imagine Nolan grew jealous and trumped up the charges against him.'

The beast seemed pensive. 'Those I represent need to know more.'

'Then ask Nolan – or Tedric – not me. I don't even know what's become of the man. He may well be dead. Nolan claims publicly that he is.'

'Nolan is incorrect. Tedric presently serves the cause of Fra Villion.'

'The pirate?' Carey had heard the name only in passing. Cut off from the immediacy of power, he took little interest in the affairs of the Empire.

'Fra Villion serves those I represent.'

'And Tedric serves Villion.' Carey pulled at his lower lip. 'But surely, you must know the truth. I thought you knew everything. You – or those you represent.'

The beast reacted unexpectedly to Carey's chiding tone. While he had anticipated a blast of anger in reply, Carey instead glimpsed a hint of genuine doubt in the beast's expression.

'Tedric's thoughts and motivations are difficult to read. He is an unknown factor in the pattern of the universe. He is an alien. He should not be here.'

'Then how did he get here?'

The question was an obvious one to ask, but the beast, hearing it, seemed to become aware that it had already spoken too openly, and perhaps revealed too much. Its face assumed the expression of a frozen mask. 'If you cannot assist us in the matter of Tedric, then we must proceed with our previous plans.'

Something in the beast's cold tone chilled Carey to the core. 'What plans?'

'Since it is absolutely necessary that we divine the genuine nature of Tedric's present loyalties, we have devised a certain test for him. It is known that Tedric loves your sister, Alyc.'

Carey laughed in what might have been surprise. He was aware that Alyc had once been held captive by the same gang of renegades that had formed the core of the insurgents who had driven him from his throne. Tedric, along with Phillip Nolan, had been a key member of that gang. 'And does she love him?'

'The question is irrelevant. To test his motives, we have ordered him to carry out her death.'

Carey stared at the beast, unable to remain entirely unmoved. Even if he hated Alyc for failing to stand with her own family during the rebellion, he did not wish her death. 'What will that prove? Tedric may be the biggest traitor in the universe and still refuse to kill Alyc.'

'We doubt that. Tedric is not an ordinary man. If he loves, he cannot serve our cause.'

'And if he kills Alyc?'

'Then he must serve us; and the others – those he was thought to serve – will have failed.'

'I see,' said Carey, though in truth he did not. 'And how do you plan to carry out this . . . this assassination?'

'Alyc makes her present home on the planet Milrod Eleven. Recently, a weapon of vast power has come into certain hands. This weapon is of a far greater destructive magnitude than any as yet known to your Empire.'

'How much greater?' Carey felt himself trembling He sensed that what the beast was about to reveal would be very disturbing indeed.

'The weapon can destroy an entire planet.'

Carey tried to laugh. 'That's absurd.'

'Is it?' the beast said sharply.

'Yes,' said Carey. 'Where did this supposed weapon come from?'

'Once every few centuries, a man of real genius must appear. More often than not, that man will be ignored, suppressed, even destroyed. His talent is simple: the ability to perceive the fabric of the cosmos with unprecedented clarity. Such a man presently exists and those whom I serve have found him. This man devised the weapon I have described to you.'

'And where is he now?'

'In space, with Tedric, on his way to Milrod Eleven.'

'Which he will destroy?'

'Which Tedric will destroy, yes.'

Carey struggled to keep the eagerness out of his voice. He didn't want the beast to realise how important this was for him. Milrod Eleven was his home, Alyc was his sister, but only one thing seemed to matter now. 'Can you obtain this weapon for my use?'

The beast laughed heartily, and Carey saw that his attempt at concealment had failed. 'So you have still not given up?' said the beast. 'You still wish to reconquer the Empire and reclaim your throne! In time, Matthew Carey, in good time. Those I represent will send me to speak with you again. First, this matter of Tedric must be settled. So long as he exists, nothing can be promised firmly.'

'But the man is a nothing!' Carey cried.

The beast winked. Carey had never seen it make such a gesture before. 'That, we hope, will soon be true.'

Then it was gone. Where it had stood, only empty air swirled. Carey staggered forward, screaming at the top of his voice, swinging his fists impotently through the air.

The door flew open. A female subman stood on the threshold, her jaw hanging open in astonishment. 'I . . . I came to do the cleaning, sir.'

'Get out!' Carey screamed. He rushed upon the cowering female, who scampered back away from him. 'I want nothing from you – nothing from anyone! Get out and stay out!' He slammed the door firmly in her face.

Turning to retrace his steps, Carey stepped squarely in the middle of the pile of goo that had once been his breakfast.

Throwing his hands high over his head, he gave vent to a desperate, angry, unrestrained wail of rage and fury.

The beast would come back. It *had* to come back.

CHAPTER 7

The Matter-Scrambler

Things were better now that he was back in space, Tedric believed. He could think more clearly, see people and events in proper perspective. He sat alone in the pilot's compartment of the small, nameless spacecraft that was hurtling him and his crew through the void at a velocity some one hundred times greater than that of light. It was only here, surrounded by the grey vacuum of N-space, far distant from the noisy, populated worlds of mankind, that a semblance of serenity entered his soul. Tedric peered through the window in front of him at the all-encompassing blankness before him. It was odd that he reacted so well to N-space. Some men, he knew, had been transformed into gibbering idiots at their first glimpse of the infinite void; but Tedric found it relaxing, not fearsome, soothing rather than maddening. Perhaps it was because he was somehow reminded of his home universe. That was a grey place, too, as well as he could recall it. Not vacant like N-space, of course, but certainly sparsely inhabited compared to the teeming planets of the Empire of Man. He could remember walking for days without passing another soul. At least he thought he could remember. It was all so dim, so vague, so dreamlike.

The ship Fra Villion had provided was an excellent machine, more than spaceworthy, a midget cruiser well-equipped for a crew of five. The forward cockpit, where he presently sat, protruded from the blimp-like frame like a bump. Yod, Ky-shan, Juvi, and Dass were in the back. Each had been assigned specific duties to perform.

Milrod Eleven was a mere four days distant. Tedric wished for more time in which to think and decide. Back on Nykzas, he had agreed to serve Fra Villion, but now that he was actually this close, only one thing stood clearly in his mind: he would never consent to harm Lady Alyc Carey.

And he was angry. Bitterly, deeply angry. But so accustomed was Tedric to concealing his real emotions that no observer, no matter how perceptive, could possibly have guessed at the rage welling up inside this tall, muscular, blond-haired man.

Specifically, Tedric was angry at Skandos of Prime, and the Scientists he represented. It was the Scientists who had brought him to this universe, to serve them in their actions against certain unspecified enemies. Until now Tedric had followed their wishes. He had served them well, risking his own life and liberty without a thought for the consequences, but now he was finally beginning to have doubts. The arrogance of the Scientists angered him. Who were they to tear a man out of his own time and universe to serve their particular ends? What did he owe them, when they refused to divulge enough information to allow him to act as anything more than their puppet? The Scientists had treated him like a child since the very beginning, and now they were demanding what he regarded as the ultimate sacrifice: they wanted him to kill Lady Alyc. Not that they had ever told him so – not in actual words, no. But her life meant nothing to them – no individual did. Fra Villion was important, Alyc was not. Fra Villion was intimately involved in the vast cosmic dispute that was raging in this universe, a dispute about which Tedric still knew next to nothing, and Alyc was merely one insignificant person. Well, he wouldn't do it. He wouldn't kill her. Neither Villion nor the Scientists could extract that price from him. He had made up his mind for certain.

And Fra Villion was a Bioman, too. If it had not been for Ky-shan, he would never have known that. And more than a Bioman, Fra Villion was a black knight, a *vemplar*, a member of a rare and special breed about whom legends still circulated hundreds of years after they had left the worlds of men. Surely the Scientists were aware of all this, and yet they had never bothered to inform him. He knew their excuses. 'We cannot intervene directly,' Standos had told him, 'for to do that would allow our adversaries the same privileges.' Tedric didn't care. He required information and assistance, and instead he was stranded here in the void of N-space with the supposed fate of the entire human race resting upon his own less-than-eager shoulders. He would have found the situation funny if it hadn't been so deadly serious.

Tedric decided to ignore the ethical questions involved and concentrate for the time being on the few hard facts at hand. Fra Villion was a Bioman, a fact that should have been of some practical value. Carefully, Tedric reviewed what little he knew of the history of that species. The Bioman race had been born on the Earth during those terrible centuries of nearly uninterrupted warfare that had raged between the time of man's first hesitant step into space and the invention of the N-space drive. Biological tactics had first led to the development of the various subman breeds, as one side or the other – it had always been difficult for Tedric to recall who was who in these complex, pointless wars – had used lower animals to replace the thousands of human beings slaughtered during the earlier phases of the conflict. The Bioman species had also emerged from the laboratory, the result of genes being deliberately manipulated towards superhuman potentiality. What the military leaders of Earth had failed to comprehend was that any such super race would not be content to play a subservient role in human affairs. It was not long, therefore, before the Biomen had wrested control of the laboratories and managed to perfect their own breed. Unwilling to rule, refusing to become involved in the human wars that swirled around them, the Biomen had lived apart, occupying a number of island satellites within the Solar System, until the invention of the N-space drive – invented, interestingly enough, by a normal human being – had allowed them finally to settle in a portion of the Galaxy far from the systems of their forebears.

Since the time of the Scattering, contact between the two species had been nearly non-existent. The Biomen bluntly refused to allow any imperial ships inside the boundaries of their realm, and while a few stray individuals, such as the robot, Wilson, had indeed managed to visit the Bioman Sphere, they had apparently learned little and revealed even less. It was said that the Biomen now existed on a separate and higher mental plane than human kind and were possessed of certain unspecified powers that made them a species truly apart. What Ky-shan had said about the ability of Biomen to project themselves through space came as no particular surprise to Tedric. He had heard other, wilder claims before. Whether any of them were true or not he didn't know. Perhaps no one knew but the Biomen themselves.

And Fra Villion was a *vemplar*, too – or at least Ky-shan thought he was. The *vemplars* were the only members of their race to take any interest in the wars of the Old Earth, selling their services to whichever warring faction was willing to make the highest bid. The *vemplars* were black knights, true warriors bred to the vocation of war, whose deeds of heroism had formed the basis of a dozen epic poems. Tedric himself had always wondered if heroism could truly be said to exist without loyalty or honour. A *vemplar* made war for the sheer pleasure of the act. His code upheld the ideal of constant conflict. And yet twice in human history, when it had appeared that the wars had gotten out of hand and the entire human race might well perish as a result, it was the *vemplars* who had intervened, putting an end to the killing until it could be resumed later on a smaller and less fatal scale.

The *vemplars* were undoubtedly a strange breed among a strange breed, and if one of them had suddenly materialised in the Empire of Man then it surely meant trouble was coming.

Wasn't it therefore his duty – Tedric's duty – to investigate the phenomenon and discover its actual meaning?

No! He slammed his fist hard into the control panel in front of him, shattering a pane of glass. It wasn't his duty, he hadn't even been born here!

Tedric looked down at his hand. A trickle of blood flowed from one knuckle. Suddenly, he laughed, a sharp bitter sound but one that made him feel instantly better. He knew what he would do, knew where his duty lay. It wasn't to abstracts, to principles. It was to the human race, to people – to his friends and companions. Above all else, it was to himself. He would do nothing contrary to the aims of his own existence, and that included not harming Lady Alyc Carey.

He thought of Yod Cartwright, in the rear of the ship. Yod had his own motives, his own desires, duties, and aims. Yod wanted Fra Villion dead just as much as the Scientists did, and with much more reason. On the trip to the spaceport, Yod had explained his own background. He had travelled from Drexon's World to Nykzas for one reason only: to kill Fra Villion. It had started several months before, when a pirate ship in search of food supplies had raided Drexon's World. The ship, it was said, was under the command of Fra Villion.

'Did you actually see it?' Juvi asked. Tedric took no part in the conversation, but listened carefully.

'No,' said Yod. 'I was out in the fields that day, supervising a team of submen who were harvesting the autumn crop. I heard something that might have been a ship, but it was a cloudy day and I didn't think anything about it. Later, I heard the noise of the heatrays.'

'Then Villion's ship attacked your farm?'

'Not the main ship, no. It struck in the city. There was a smaller shuttle. It landed, took what it could find, and then left.'

'And you never actually saw them?'

'I couldn't get there fast enough.'

'Then how do you know Villion was there?'

'I don't. But they were his men. Who else can I blame?'

'Did they burn your home?'

He nodded grimly. 'Yes.'

'Is that all?'

'No.' His voice had grown soft.

'What?'

'They killed my family, all of them – even my kid brother. I found the bodies . . . they burned some of them; my two sisters had been . . .'

Juvi said, 'I'm sorry, Yod, I didn't mean –'

He interrupted her, lifting his head and nearly shouting. 'And that's why I have to kill him. It's either him or me. Do you understand?'

Juvi started to say that she did, but Tedric intervened first. 'It doesn't make sense to me,' he said.

'Yod looked at him as if he were crazy. 'Didn't you hear what I just said?'

Tedric nodded. 'I was listening, but I still don't understand. You won't kill Villion – he'll kill you. How will that help your parents or your brothers and sisters? They're already dead. Your dying, too, won't bring them back.'

'And what makes you so sure I won't kill Villion?'

Tedric sighed. He already felt disturbed because of Villion's order concerning the destruction of Milrod Eleven, and Yod's youthful naïvety was only an additional irritation. 'Because he's already given you an opportunity to survive and you refused to take it. You tried to kill him once. He's not going to forget that. Do you think Villion's the forgiving type? Well, he isn't. He just wanted to be sure you represented a genuine threat before taking action. If you'd refused to join the rest of us, he'd have gladly let you live, but since you said yes, he's got to assume you're determined to try again. He'll have to kill you. As soon as we reach wherever it is we're going, I imagine he'll act.'

'I'm willing to take that chance,' Yod said stoically, but his voice was hollow. Tedric's logic was impeccable and even Yod realised that. Still, he remained determined to proceed even if, by doing so, he doomed himself to almost certain death. In a way, Tedric admired and envied the boy. In another way, he thought him an outright fool.

But Yod had his own good reasons for acting as he did. He was driven by his own established interests, by a private need for revenge. Tedric regretted that his own life could not be that simple. He wished he could chase Villion because he hated him and not because of some vast, unspecified plan to save an entire universe.

Standing, Tedric began to pace. As far as he could see, only one option made real sense. The fact was that he had indeed once promised Skandos and the Scientists that he would serve their interests. His entire life in this universe up until now had been predicated upon that promise. If he backed out now, everything he had accomplished these past few years would be rendered meaningless. So he was willing to proceed. He would continue to fight Fra Villion, and anyone else who crossed his path, until such time as something could finally be settled.

But what of Alyc? He knew he would not harm her. Nothing – including the need to have meaning in his own life – was worth that. It was a predicament. He had decided to fight Villion, but doing that necessitated destroying Milrod Eleven and Alyc Carey with it. Which should he do? Kill Alyc and continue on to Villion's headquarters? Or spare Alyc and thus throw away all that had been accomplished the last few months? The decision facing him was the same as when he had been on Nykzas. He had delayed choosing then, hoping perhaps for a miracle. That miracle had not happened. Not yet, anyway.

Tedric spoke softly to the ship's computer. 'Give me our estimated time of rendezvous with Milrod Eleven.'

A few seconds passed. There was a clicking sound. Tedric reached out and read the typed reply: *three days, nineteen hours, fifty-eight minutes, four seconds.*

He smiled bitterly. There was still time – time for a miracle.

He decided to talk to Milton Dass. After all, the matter-scrambler, the cause of his whole dilemma, was Dass's creation. He went into the back. Dass was not there. Juvi, who was helping Ky-shan monitor the engines, told him to look in Dass's room.

'Was he excused from duty?'

'I think he's spacesick.'

Tedric found Dass lying in his bunk. The viewport above his head had been covered with a blanket, and Dass's face was as pale as the rays of a distant star. When Tedric shut the door softly behind him, Dass shifted on his bed and moaned.

'I'd like to talk to you for a moment, Milton,' Tedric said.

Dass turned his head rigidly. 'What about? I'm sick. Can't you see that? I'm dying.'

Tedric grinned. 'You'll be all right in time.'

'I don't think so,' Dass said stubbornly. 'Space is a horrendous place. I don't see how you can bear it. Look at this floor. Do you have any idea how thick it is? Three metres. That's all. If something happened, if it cracked, a person could fall through and never stop. N-space is truly infinite. I can prove that mathematically. You could fall forever.'

Tedric laughed. 'You wouldn't fall anywhere,' he said. 'But I know what you mean. Try not to think about it.'

'I can't seem to think of anything else,' Dass said.

Tedric was not entirely unsympathetic to Dass's predicament. He had seen similarly afflicted men in the past and knew that N-spacesickness was a problem that might strike anyone. During his intial year at the Academy of the Corps of the One Hundred, the most promising cadet in his class had been a young man named Dav Ryan, whose father and grandfather before him had served with distinction in the Corps. Everyone anticipated great success for Ryan, but when the time came for his initial solo flight through N-space, Ryan's career suddenly ended. He was struck utterly and hopelessly spacesick, too ill even to pilot his own craft. He had gone home the very next day. The problem with N-space was that it was really a madman's realm. Anyone who thought about it – truly thought about it – just couldn't bear it.

'I'd like to talk to you about the matter-scrambler,' Tedric said.

'Well, what do you want to know? I can give you the mathematics, but that's really about all.' It was clearly a struggle for him to speak, but thinking of something besides the infinite void a bare three metres away did seem to help.

'What about the theory? Can you tell me how it works?'

'I suppose I can try.' Dass licked his lips. A trickle of sweat ran down his cheeks. 'It's really not complicated. All matter is composed of atoms. My matter-scrambler causes the atoms to repel each other. The result is immediate and total destruction.'

'And this works on living as well as non-living matter?'

Dass nodded. 'The matter-scrambler cannot make a distinction. As far as it's concerned, an atom is an atom.'

'Then you are aware that you've created the most destructive weapon in human history.'

'I have to be aware.' He spoke slowly, fitfully, with an element of reluctance in his voice.

'You talk as if you're not happy about it.'

'Would you be? I was playing mathematical games, that's all. Then Villion came to me. It was his idea to build a weapon. I wanted to help people, not kill them.'

This was a different Milton Dass from the one Tedric had met in the big mansion on Nykzas. The spasmodic flow of his genius had faded, and it wasn't because of illness. 'Then why did you do it?'

Dass turned his eyes around the room as if he felt they were being watched. 'Villion ordered me not to tell.'

'He can't hear you. I carry a gadget that counteracts any listening device.'

'What does it matter, I'll tell you anyway.' Dass sat up and looked bitterly at Tedric. 'He stole my wife. I loved her, and he took her away.'

'He kidnapped her?'

'I – yes. Oh, I don't know. All I know is she went with him. He took her to this place where we're going now, and he told me she'd never come back unless I did as he asked.'

Tedric frowned. He hated coercion no matter what form it took. Everyone possessed the basic right to choose the direction of their own life. 'Then he blackmailed you?'

'I suppose you could call it that. He lived in my house, haunted it like a ghost, and then one day both of them were gone – him and Lola – and only he came back.'

'Was it Villion himself – or just a projection?'

'No, it was the real thing then.'

'And he made you build the matter-scrambler?'

'Yes.'

'And now he intends to blow up a whole world?'

'I know,' Dass said bleakly, 'but what can I do? What can anyone do? You're on his side. What should you care?'

Tedric edged away. Dass was right. There was no way he could answer these questions without revealing more than he wished about his own motives. 'Stay here,' he told Dass, 'until you feel better. Then report for duty. It won't be long before we get to where we're going.'

'I know,' said Dass. He didn't sound pleased by the prospect.

Tedric went back to the cockpit and stood, staring out the window. I won't do it, he thought. If they want it done – if Skandos wants it done – then he's going to have to show me how.

He sat down in the pilot's chair.

CHAPTER 8

On Milrod Eleven

Lady Alyc Carey knelt in a patch of soft grass in the well-tended garden that surrounded the house she now occupied alone on the family planet Milrod Eleven; she was thinking about the things she had seen when she had accompanied Tedric into space to observe the red morass of the alien cloud.

Seen. That was the word she used, and that was how she felt. She had *seen* the red cloud, even though, for more than half her life, she had been totally blind.

Blind, yes – she conceded that – but sightless? No, never, for Lady Alyc had come to realise that sight consisted of much more than one organ, one sense. Those who limited their sight to what their eyes captured were far blinder than she herself ever could be.

The accident that had blinded her had taken place when she was only a small child, and her remembrance of the time before, when her eyes still worked, was limited to a few stray flashes that came to her mostly as she dreamed. It didn't matter. She didn't need to remember. She knew what it was like to see. Her father, Melor Carey, had been the single most powerful man in the Empire, but the one person he had never learned to command was his only daughter; and when Alyc asked to join him aboard the family yacht *Blue Eagle*, which was going into space to observe the impending nova of the star KC 97L, he had not known how to refuse.

Not that she blamed him. Her father had never been a kind man, or even a good man, but he had never intended her any direct harm. If she blamed anyone for the accident that destroyed her eyesight, it was herself, and she preferred not to do that either, for self-hatred was ultimately pointless; she had long since ceased to hate at all.

Even now, she could not remember the moment of blindness without feeling pain. The agony was indescribable, like a hot knife slicing the naked eye. And they had certainly warned her. Time and again, her father and his crew had said, don't look, don't even peek. When that star goes, watch on the screens and only the screens.

She hadn't believed them. Either that or else her own arrogance had somehow convinced her that what might injure another could never possibly harm the daughter of Melor Carey. So she had opened the porthole. Just an inch. Just to peek. It seeemed so absurd to come this far and then see nothing more than what might later be glimpsed on a tridee newstape.

Just as she turned her eyes to the porthole, star KC97L went nova.

And Alyc Carey was struck instantly blind.

The finest surgeons in the Empire of Man laboured for months to regain her eyesight.

They failed.

Alyc went home to Milrod Eleven, where her father maintained a home on an otherwise uninhabited planet. She was given a maidservant, a subwoman named Kisha, descended from lions. There was a robot, Kuevee, who tended the garden where various plants and forms of vegetation from a hundred different star systems existed in paradoxical harmony. Her older brother Matthew visited occasionally from Earth. Otherwise, she lived alone. Her father thought it was right – safer. Alyc thought he was wrong. More than anything else, she longed to be free. She wanted to see – though without benefit of eyes – the Galaxy she knew existed out there. When she was nineteen, she at last managed to convince her father to permit her a brief escape from Milrod Eleven. Accompanied by Kisha, she booked passage aboard the spaceliner *Oceania*, scheduled to visit eighteen planets on a round trip of nine months duration.

The *Oceania* was only partway through its journey, however, when it was intercepted and boarded by a band of space pirates. When the pirates discovered who Alyc Carey was, they decided to make her their prisoner. She did not resist them. As a matter of fact, so thoroughly bored was she with her life, that she actually encouraged them. The pirates were more than mere brigands. One of their leaders, Phillip Nolan, was a man of high birth whose family had once held the same high imperial position now occupied by the Careys. When she returned with the pirates to their home base, the invisible planet Quicksilver, she learned that their primary interest wasn't mere piracy – it was also revolution. Her brother Matthew had recently crowned himself Emperor. The pirates wished to restore the throne to its proper heir, Prince Randow. Alyc disliked her older brother thoroughly and was not entirely unsympathetic to the pirates' aims.

Another of the pirate leaders – in fact, their true leader, though most of them failed to realise the fact – was Tedric. She found out that Tedric was a tall, heavily built, thickly muscled young man, with long blond hair and an expression of fierce determination. Tedric had once been Lord Tedric of the Marshes. Alyc had heard that name long before she had ever met him. She had heard it from her voices.

More than likely, the same cosmic explosion that had robbed her of her eyesight had simultaneously granted her this strange power. She heard voices constantly, sometimes loud, sometimes distant. At first she had assumed she was crazy and told no one. Until Tedric. And Tedric hadn't thought she was crazy at all.

The voices that she heard, he believed, consisted of the telepathic conversation of the Scientists of Prime. That was why she had heard them speak his name, because the Scientists of Prime had brought Tedric to this universe from his home to serve certain purposes of their own.

But she heard two sets of voices, not one. She told Tedric about the second. These voices were of ugly, monstrous things speaking constantly of death and suffering. When she heard them, she could barely keep from screaming aloud. These second voices were fainter and less frequent. They seemed to come from a farther distance. But when she heard them, she never forgot them.

Tedric said he thought he knew what these voices represented, too. There are at least two great opposing forces in conflict in our universe, he told her. The Scientists are one, but they have an adversary. The ugly voices you hear must come from those beings.

She believed him. All at once, relieved of her fears of madness, she felt very much like a free person. She fell in love with Lord Tedric of the Marshes, too. He didn't know it – but she had.

Later, she had stood close by his side during the cataclysmic space battle between the imperial fleet and the rebel forces that had eventually ended in complete victory for the rebels. She had gone to Earth to watch the coronation of Emperor Randow. And then she had returned to Milrod. Her father had died on Earth during the brief reign of his son. She was alone now, except for Kisha and Kuevee. Alone on a planet big enough to hold a billion men.

But Tedric had come to her. And when he had, she had found herself unwilling to spend another moment alone; she had convinced him to let her accompany him on his present mission, and so the two of them – along with his Wykzl servant, Ky-shan, and her own subwoman, Kisha – had travelled through space to the corner of the Empire where the red cloud lay. Alyc had only been there a few minutes when she reached over and tugged at Tedric's sleeve. 'It was sent here by those adversaries,' she said. 'I can sense it. There's almost a stench, like death and decay.'

Eventually, when there was nothing else to learn, it had been necessary for both of them to come back. She had wished to remain with Tedric then, and he had acceded to her wishes to the extent of taking her on a tour of the scenic places in the Empire of Man; but finally, after speaking to Phillip Nolan on Earth, he came and told her that it was time for him to leave. Again, she asked to accompany him, but this time he refused. His next mission was both dangerous and secret and he would have to go alone. She objected, though not strenuously, and he insisted, though not harshly, and in the end he agreed to spend a final week with her on Milrod Eleven in the house made of glass. And then he left, promising to return as soon as possible.

She had soon heard about Tedric's arrest and exile, and his eventual escape, but took none of that seriously. She knew Tedric was not a traitor. All of this was obviously part of the secret assignment he had mentioned to her.

Above her head, the raw yellow sun had reached its zenith in the cloudless blue-pink sky. She could feel the heat of midday pounding on her skull and, sighing languorously, she leaned back, tilted her face towards the soothing rays and wondered, not for the first time, why so many people seemed to feel the need of two eyes in order to see. 'Kisha,' she said. 'Kisha, are you here?'

'Yes, Alyc.' There was the familiar warm touch of the sub-woman's soft hand.

'Kisha, I think I feel him nearby.'

'Who, Alyc?'

'Lord Tedric.'

'But wouldn't he let us know?'

'Perhaps he cannot. Perhaps . . .' She paused, letting her words die unspoken. She had never hinted to Kisha about her voices, but it was the good voices, the Scientists, who had first given her the idea that Tedric might be coming. They had spoken of him recently, and although the actual meaning of their words was sometimes difficult to decipher, she had learned enough to realise that Tedric was engaged on a particularly dangerous and delicate mission.

But now she was certain he was coming. It was more than just the voices. She could sense his presence, feel him drawing near.

And something was wrong.

'Kuevee,' she said. 'Are you here?' The gentle squeaking of the robot's wheels turning in the soft mud of the garden had alerted her to its presence.

'Yes, Alyc.'

'Would you come here? Stand closer. I want both you and Kisha near me for the moment.'

'Is something wrong?' asked Kisha, drawing suddenly back. She, too, could see with something greater than her eyes. She was a cat, great-granddaughter of a lion, and possessed the sixth sense of such beasts.

'No, of course not,' said Alyc, with an effort at lightness. She was not telling the truth. A new and terrible emotion now swept through her. It was Tedric, all right. He was trying to speak, trying to warn her.

'You're pale,' said Kisha. 'It's this sun. You shouldn't sit out here and be – '

'*No.*' She spoke too sharply, but the feeling was growing, the feeling of danger; it was stronger than ever. 'Don't move away. Stay here. Stay close.'

'Alyc, what's wrong?'

In the big house, an alarm sounded. Alyc sat up stiffly, holding Kisha tight. Her father had once installed a robot alarm system to warn of any approaching alien ship. 'That's Tedric,' she said, knowing positively that the ship was his and yet not comprehending this emotion, this fear. 'I don't know why he – '

She didn't speak again. Just then, just as her lips moved to utter another word, it happened.

The atoms that composed the human mind and body that was Lady Alyc Carey shattered.

And, where the planet Milrod Eleven had once floated in the void of space, there was now nothing to be seen.

CHAPTER 9

The Scientists

Skandos, the histro-physicist, sat crosslegged on the summit of Prime's tallest mountain, wreathed in clouds and oblivious to the blanket of snow beneath him. His arms were folded stoically across his chest as he watched the incorporeal forms of several of his colleagues buzzing angrily around him.

'What you did was not only wrong, it was foolish,' proclaimed one, Aalban, an archeobiologist noted for his nervous ways. 'You have risked all our plans, the fate of the known universe, without consulting with anyone else.'

To converse it was not necessary for the Scientists to use the traditional tools of lips, tongue, and throat. They spoke directly to one another, mind-to-mind, in a language more dependent upon mood and symbol than mere words.

'I consulted with no one because it was not necessary,' said Skandos in his own defence. 'I brought Tedric to this universe and understand his thought processes better than anyone. The decision to act was mine to make, and I made it.'

'And you erred.' This was Jorken, the most vocal of Skandos's critics. A relatively young Scientist, probably not more than three or four thousand years old, Jorken excited easily. He suddenly assumed a material form and dropped to the snow beside Skandos. His wiry red hair stood stiffly out on his skull. 'Tedric is a barbarian. He must serve our demands.'

'But he is also a man and he has a will of his own,' Skandos answered patiently. 'Had I failed to act when I did, we would have forsaken his crucial assistance forever.'

'Then that is a risk that should have been taken,' said

Jorken. 'Is his assistance worth the price of intervention?'

'I believed that it was, and I have the figures to prove it. If you wish, I would be pleased to share my calculations with you.' He was being sardonic. Skandos was well aware that none of them could possibly understand the methods of histrophysics. 'Without Tedric, our own hopes are doomed to fail. The adversaries will emerge triumphant and the universe will suffer a slow death.'

'One mere barbarian is so important?' Jorken said derisively. 'Surely, you cannot expect us to believe such an absurd claim.'

'Believe it or not, Jorken, it is true. Mathematics do not lie.'

'Nor do they tell all of the truth. You yourself have admitted that this Tedric is not a directable force. With the liberty you have granted him, no one can possibly predict his subsequent actions.'

'Nor are they important.' Skandos spoke with a calmness at odds with the irritation he felt. He intended to treat Jorken and the others as ignorant students of universal politics. 'Tedric is a catalyst. His presence in our universe is the crucial component that permits victory over our adversaries to be considered as a possibility.'

'Then how could he dare to refuse to serve us?' This was a new voice, Dallia, a female psychologist.

'Because, above all else, Tedric is a free man. You of all people should understand that, Dallia.'

'Dallia may, but I do not,' Jorken said, still on the offensive.

Skandos fought to remain serene. 'Tedric's only value to us derives from his status as a free man but, as such, he is capable of forming his own decisions. Tedric believed we were asking him to destroy someone he had come to love. In all good conscience, as a free man, he refused to do that.'

'Love,' Jorken said, his voice welling up with contempt. 'How can you permit something so foolish to stand in the face of a conflict that threatens to engulf the universe?'

'Because, to the one involved, love may seem far more important. Even you were once a mortal man, Jorken. Didn't you ever fall in love? Which was more important to you? The person you loved or an abstract equation? Tedric can see and touch Lady Alyc Carey. He has not yet met our adversaries.'

'Then how can you place so much power and authority in the hands of such a person? It is the problem with all mortals. They have never learned to focus upon the eternal questions and ignore the transitory.'

'That is because, to them, the transitory is of more importance.'

'And that is their crucial failing.'

Skandos shook his head. He was weary of this discussion. Jorken was too dogmatic. That was his crucial failing, and to Skandos, it was a handicap much more debilitating than love. 'I believe that I acted best. Milton Dass invented the matter-scrambler with no assistance from me.'

Jorken moved in quickly, like a shark smelling blood. 'And that is exactly why I demanded this present discussion. Your famous calculations, upon which we have based so much of our effort, insisted that no such break-through in weaponry could occur for several more centuries. You were wrong, Skandos, your calculations were mistaken, and you intervened directly in order to cover up the failure of your own devices.'

Skandos sighed softly to himself. As the only histro-physicist presently active among the Scientists, it was always a trial to explain to the others exactly how his science worked. 'Milton Dass is a genius and, as such, not subject to the flow of scientific history. I could no more predict his appearance at this point in time than you could predict the exact moment when a meteor might strike this mountain.'

'The chances of that ever occurring are infinitesimal.'

'As were the chances of the matter-scrambler being invented now. But it happened, and I do not believe I acted unwisely in making available a temporary defence.'

The debate had returned to Aalban once again. The doubts he expressed were common to all of them and the real reason for this meeting today. 'If our adversaries find out how you have intervened, they may very well decide to take a similar step. That is why we have all agreed to do nothing before now. The risk of escalation is not worth the possible advantage we have briefly attained.'

'It is my opinion,' Skandos said, well aware of the impact his words were certain to make, 'that the adversaries have long since intervened in this conflict in ways more direct and substantial than any we have ever contemplated.'

It was Jorken who interrupted the tense silence. 'Perhaps you should be specific. What are you talking about?'

'Fra Villion,' Skandos said, 'and the red clouds. What else did you think?'

Even Jorken said nothing this time. Skandos had maliciously reminded his colleagues of matters they preferred to forget. He felt no pity for them. They claimed to object to the fact that he had chosen to save Alyc Carey from the blast of the matter-scrambler, but the degree of intervention involved was minute compared to the adversaries and their red clouds. Jorken and the others were simply frightened. Skandos, realising this, felt something like contempt for them.

Then Zorza spoke. He was the oldest and wisest of all the Scientists. A psycho-philosopher, Zorza had last offered an opinion some ten thousand years before. What he now said was simple: 'Skandos has done the right thing.'

The others said nothing. None dared to challenge Zorza.

'But he is also wrong,' Zorza went on. 'All of us are. We have treated Tedric as if he were nothing more than a minor player in a vast cosmic game of chess. He is more than that. Tedric is a man. Skandos believes that because it is possible to chart the probabilities, history is merely a science, but it is more than that. History is an art, part of which is the creation of men; and men are individuals, each distinct and separate. Tedric came to our universe not to be a puppet, not to follow our dictates, but to be himself. Skandos was correct in intervening because Tedric had asked him to do so. We are his servants. He is the master. Our adversaries can never understand this; in the end, therefore, they must fail.'

'Do you have any calculations to back that up?' cried Jorken, but the others ignored his youthful rudeness. They understood that Zorza was right, and they felt shamed.

Skandos turned away. This petty bickering was gaining

nothing. Even now, with Milrod Eleven behind him, Tedric was approaching the pirate base.

Skandos wanted to be alone. He wanted to watch and observe. If Tedric was the master, then Skandos was eager to serve.

CHAPTER 10

Into the Iron Sphere

Tedric shook his head at the awesome sight that filled the middle of the cockpit window. Lowering his eyes, he could see the same view reflected in the screen on the control panel, but it seemed less impressive: the crystalline scarlet sheen of the red cloud certainly loomed large, but in the window even that huge shape was nearly obscured by the round black object floating in front of it.

'What is it?' asked a soft voice close to his elbow. It was Juvi. As soon as the computer had signalled their imminent departure from N-space, he had called the others forward to observe. He didn't know what he had expected them to see. Certainly not this.

'Whatever it is, there's someone aboard it.'

'How can you be sure?'

'Can you see those smaller shapes at the edge of the screen?'

She looked to where he was pointing. 'They look like insects, flies circling a rotten fruit.'

'They're ships – as big as ours.'

'Then that sphere must be really huge!'

'It is.' Tedric estimated the diameter of the round object at nearly forty kilometres. 'Bigger than any ship I've ever seen.'

'Ship?' said Yod Cartwright, who was standing close to Tedric's other side. 'It's a planet, isn't it?'

'No. It's too round and too smooth. There are such things as wandering planets, but this isn't one of them. This is artificial.'

'Who built it?' said Juvi.

'Until we learn otherwise, we've got to assume Fra Villion. He's the one who brought us here.'

'Tedric,' said a voice from the rear of the cockpit. This was Ky-shan, crouched above the navigational instruments.

He turned, almost in relief, glad to fix his eyes upon something other than that dark spectre ahead. 'Yes, what is it?'

'I've got a reading on our own course. We're heading directly towards the sphere. Rendezvous in twenty minutes.'

'Could you pull us away if you wanted?'

'No. The computer has assumed complete control.'

Tedric smiled faintly. 'Then I suppose all we can do is sit back and relax. Our fate is out of our hands.'

'It appears so, yes.'

Milton Dass was peering at the window with an intense, calculating expression on his face. 'I can see it spinning,' he announced. 'Whatever it is, it's rotating like a planet.'

'But isn't this the same as Nexus, where the Corps has its cadet academy?' Yod asked. 'That's an artificial planet, too, isn't it?'

'Nexus isn't a twentieth of this size,' said Juvi.

'This world is larger than most asteroids and many satellites,' Dass said. His spacesickness seemed well under control, and yet his mood remained morose. He had hardly spoken a word since they had left the region of Milrod Eleven.

'But what's that other thing in the background?' Juvi said. 'That red thing. It looks almost like a cloud.'

'It is a cloud,' Tedric said.

'I've never seen a dust cloud of that consistency before,' Dass said. 'It looks almost solid.'

'There are a lot of peculiar things in space,' Tedric said, with a casual shrug. He saw no purpose in explaining to these people exactly how peculiar – and deadly – the red cloud really was.

The ship slowed noticeably as it drew closer to the object ahead. Since Tedric had visited this part of space in the recent past, he was fairly certain that the iron sphere had not been present at that time. Or had it? The ship he had personally ordered to monitor the cloud was undoubtedly still in the vicinity. Why hadn't it reported sighting this giant ship?

Tedric realised that he was allowing his present situation to distort his perceptions. Seen from here, the object appeared huge, but against the vastness of space it was still quite insignificant.

The ship had not reported the sphere because it had never noticed it.

The artificial world now filled the entire span of the window. Their ship edged forward, drifting towards eventual rendezvous. The surface of the sphere seemed as smooth as a ball. A square gap opened in the upper hemisphere and a measure of light glimmered through. Tedric could see the pinpricks of the stars reflected on the mirror-like face of the object. The ship headed towards the gap. Tedric made no effort to steer, trusting to the programmed wisdom of the computer. The ship glided forward. The window showed a gash of yellow light. Then they were inside. The ship stopped.

There was a loud clang against the outer hull.

'I think they're asking us to come out,' Tedric said, turning to face the others.

'I'm ready,' said Yod, drawing himself to his full height and resting his hand on the butt of his heatgun.

Tedric thought of asking for the weapon, but decided that it wasn't really his business. He was certain Fra Villion could protect himself and that, by doing so, he would probably protect Yod as well. 'Then let's go,' he said.

Only Milton Dass hung back. 'Do you think I ought to bring . . . ?'

'No, leave it.' Dass was referring to the newly disassembled matter-scrambler. 'If Villion wants the weapon, he can come and get it.'

Tedric cycled the lock. A tubular plastic tunnel had been fastened to the outside of the door, and the five of them walked along it to another door. A man was waiting for them on the other side. He saluted with a crispness that was almost military. 'In the name of Fra Villion, I welcome you to the bastion of the Iron Sphere.'

Tedric saluted in return. The others stayed back. 'Is that what you call it?'

The man nodded. 'Yes, this is Fra Villion's headquarters. I am Lieutenant Galton. You are Tedric?'

'I am.' He introduced Yod, Juvi, Ky-shan, and Dass. He wondered how Galton had come to be designated a lieutenant. In dress, bearing, and attitude, he resembled any other unemployed drifter on a backworld planet.

'If you'll come with me,' Galton said crisply, 'I'll take you below.'

The trip was long and arduous. They moved down wide brightly-lit corridors and climbed tall, dizzying staircases. Clearly, the Iron Sphere was well organised. The creatures they passed – mostly men and submen but including a number of aliens, too – paused long enough to salute Galton, whom they apparently recognised. There was an air of discipline about this place, and Tedric was impressed by the manner in which Fra Villion had managed to establish authority over such a motley crew of pirates.

Lieutenant Galton provided some explanation as he guided them deeper into the core of the Sphere. 'Everyone here respects Fra Villion. He requires that all spoils be divided equally among the crew. I can't speak for the others, but I've never been wealthier in my life.'

'It must be pretty hard to spend it here.'

Galton shrugged. 'That will come in time. Villion has plans – big plans.'

'Such as what?'

Galton shook his head. 'I'm only a lieutenant. He doesn't confide in me.'

'But you have seen him?'

Suddenly ill-at-ease, Galton said, 'Well, not exactly.'

'You've seen his image?'

'Yes.'

'But he is aboard.'

'I – I suppose so. I never thought he couldn't be. Why do you ask?'

Tedric smiled. 'I was just wondering. With all that wealth on board, I'm surprised nobody has ever gotten greedy. A mutiny isn't an impossible thing among pirates.'

Galton shook his head firmly. 'Here it would have to be.

The Sphere, the ships, everything is programmed. Harm Villion and we'd all be stranded here forever. Unless the Corps found us first.'

'Does that worry you?'

'Not especially. We have the Iron Sphere, plus nearly two thousand ships of the line. As soon as Villion gives the order to move, we'll cut through the Empire in a single sweep.'

'Two thousand ships?' Tedric was surprised. The imperial navy itself – including the Corps – had only ten times that number. Villion had been busy.

'Plus the Sphere. Villion's been building three ships a day since well before I came here. If he wanted to wait, he could have twice that many. But the imperial navy has nothing like the Sphere, nothing at all.'

The Iron Sphere, it appeared, was indeed a marvellous creation. If Fra Villion was a Bioman, that helped explain the Sphere's origin, but it did not explain why it had suddenly appeared here. For centuries, the Biomen had ignored the existence of their creators. Why had they – or at least one of them – decided to intervene in human affairs now?

'How did you get here?' Tedric asked Galton. They had entered a crowded elevator, and were now dropping even further below the surface. 'Did Fra Villion recruit you?'

'Not personally, of course not, but he does have a network of agents across the Empire. With the Great Revolt, a lot of men were put out of work. I used to oversee a crew of cane-pickers on Jaybo Seventeen. After Randow declared an end to subman slave labour, I was out of a job.'

'Is that where most of these people came from?'

'A lot, sure, but not all. There are always plenty of out-of-work spacehands on any backworld planet. Villion's men talk to them about coming here, put them on a ship, and once they're here on the Iron Sphere, there's no way they can go back home.'

'I don't suppose you could tell me approximately how many men are here.' The more information he could get out of the talkative Galton the better, Tedric thought.

'Why not?' The elevator stopped with a sudden jerk and, as the doors opened on another bare corridor, Galton waved at them to disembark. 'About three hundred and eighty,' he said, as they stepped out together.

'So few?' Tedric had expected more, considering the vast size of the Sphere, and the sudden disappearance of men from backwater worlds was hardly the sort of thing to alert the Corps.

'You don't need many,' said Galton. 'The Sphere is automated. All we have to do is push buttons and the Empire is in our hands.'

Tedric lapsed into a thoughtful silence. Behind him, he could hear Juvi and Yod engaged in excited chatter about some private matter. Their voices were too high. Turning, Tedric glared at them. He could well understand, though. Excitement had that effect on some people. It made them talk about everything except what was really worrying them.

Galton motioned them to a halt in front of a tall wooden door. 'I was told to bring Tedric here and take the rest of you to your rooms. Tedric, I'll be back shortly and show you where you'll be staying.'

Tedric nodded, wondering what surprise he was about to discover behind this door. Galton had given no hint. Of the others, only Yod seemed hesitant to depart, but in the end even he went away with Galton. Once the group was out of sight, Tedric knocked on the door.

A firm voice from within told him to enter.

The room was spacious and plush and would not have seemed out of place in the imperial palace on New Melbourne. There was a thick carpet and an ornate lamp that hung from the ceiling by a chain of sparkling crystal links. Seated in a deep chair, his heels propped on a flat table, was a man Tedric knew well. It was Matthew Carey, the former Emperor.

Carey raised his eyes and smiled at Tedric. Tedric felt a moment's hate for the man, but his senses and emotions were dulled and he remained impassive. 'You act as if you expected to find me here,' said Carey after a moment; his familiar drawling voice always seemed to contain an edge of sarcasm. 'Don't tell me that idiot Galton spoiled my surprise.'

Tedric shook his head, keeping his expression studiously blank. He was not so much surprised as uneasy. Carey's presence here, however it might be explained, was not a favourable omen. His wisest course now, he decided, was to say as little as possible and force Carey to expose his own hand. 'He told me nothing,' Tedric said.

'Then who did? Aren't you a little bit intrigued? Puzzled?'

Tedric moved deeper into the room so that his substantial height loomed over the seated Carey. 'I didn't expect to find you among these pirates, no.'

'Or me, you. After all, I thought you and Phil Nolan were the best of friends.'

'We pretended to be that, yes.'

'So what happened?'

Tedric decided to stick to the cover story, that had brought him this far. 'My success worried him. I emerged from the revolution a greater hero than he. Nolan viewed me as a rival to his command of the Corps.'

'The charge was made that you plotted to put me back on my throne.'

Tedric doubted that Carey was sufficiently gullible to accept that. Treachery and jealousy were crucial aspects of his world view, but men could act only from selfish motives. 'That was the excuse he used to get rid of me.'

Carey laughed heartily, as though the two had shared a private joke. 'That's Nolan, all right. I've known him since we were both boys. Don't trust him. I think I told you that when we were both cadets. Remember?'

Tedric nodded. 'I should have listened to you then.'

Nolan shifted in his chair, dropping his feet to the carpet with a thud. 'Are you wondering what I'm doing here?'

Tedric shrugged casually. 'What are you doing here?'

'Want to guess?'

'It really doesn't interest me that much.' Tedric let an edge of irritation show in his voice as he spoke.

Carey laughed, apparently in genuine admiration. 'You are a cool customer, aren't you? I think Nolan had the right idea. You may not have a family, or much of any breeding, but you're certainly dangerous. A man doesn't come as far as you have, starting from absolutely nothing, without learning how to shove people out of the way. My grandfather was the same way.

My father, too. They knew what they wanted and went out and got it. That's why our family succeeded when the Nolans failed. We were tough and they weren't.'

'Did you ask me in here to discuss your family history?'

Carey looked shocked by such directness. It was obvious he was not accustomed to being addressed in that way. Still, after a moment's hesitation, he grinned. 'I like you, Tedric. In a place like this, there's no reason for you to treat me with deference, so you don't bother. Back at the Academy, it was different.'

'Back at the Academy, you hadn't lost a revolution yet.'

'How true. I gambled everything and I lost. It was my father's idea to begin with, you know. When old Kane killed himself, he decided to make me Emperor. That was a mistake, the only one he ever made in his life. We should have taken young Randow under our wing and ruled the same as before. If that had happened, we'd still be running the Empire – or I would.'

'And instead you're a space pirate, a running man.' Tedric, deflecting the conversation back towards the present moment, was pleased to see the flush that spread across Carey's face.

'Is that what you think I am?'

'It's what this place is all about, isn't it?'

Carey shook his head. 'Superficially, perhaps, but that's not why I'm here. I'm no *pirate.* I'm here to reclaim the Empire that you and Nolan stole from me.'

Tedric laughed aloud. 'Is that all? We'll do it after dinner.'

Carey didn't smile. 'With your help, we might even do that. Fra Villion tells me you arrived here with a very valuable cargo.'

'The matter-scrambler,' agreed Tedric, suddenly less amused by Carey.

'The most significant advance in space weaponry in a dozen centuries. The imperial navy and the Corps of the One Hundred will never stand against it.'

'They have shields. Dass admits that will provide some protection.'

'But you can't shield an entire planet. I know what you did to my old home, Milrod Eleven.'

'I acted on Fra Villion's orders.'

'I never suggested you didn't, but I was surprised. I thought you and my sister were good friends.'

'Alyc couldn't do me much good – not out here.'

For a moment even Carey looked shocked by Tedric's callousness, but then he leaned back in his chair, and smiled as he seemed to appraise Tedric anew. 'So that was what was behind it all the time? You're a man who covers all bets, aren't you, Tedric. If Nolan won the revolution, he was a good friend of yours, but if I beat him, then my sister was your lover. I'm impressed.'

'I suppose you could look at it that way,' Tedric said, with deliberate evasiveness. Some lies were more painful to maintain than others.

'You made only one minor miscalculation.' Carey went on. 'I never cared much for Alyc. I won't say I'm glad she's dead – after all, she was my sister – but I don't find that I grieve over her passing very much, either.'

'She could certainly be difficult to get along with.'

'You can say that again. You and Fra Villion ought to get along famously. I never thought anyone could have less of a heart than me, until I met Villion.'

'Then he really does exist?'

Carey looked surprised. 'You doubt it?'

'When I first saw you here, I did. I never thought you were one to take orders from someone else.'

'I'm not, but Villion is different.'

'How so?'

Carey shook his head. It was plain that he wasn't about to be lured into speaking too freely of Villion. 'You've met him. You should know.'

'I've seen his image – that's all.'

Carey frowned. 'That's all anyone has ever seen.'

'Then maybe he doesn't actually exist.'

Tedric had meant his suggestion as a joke, but Carey seemed willing to regard it solemnly. 'That's always possible, I suppose.'

There was a knock on the door. Carey did not seem displeased by the interruption. 'Enter,' he called.

It was Lieutenant Galton. 'I wanted to see if Commander

Tedric was ready to go to his room.'

'Commander?' said Tedric, lifting his brows in surprise.

'Fra Villion has a passion for military discipline,' Carey said. 'I'm a captain myself.'

'Then if you don't mind, sir, perhaps I should go and see where I'm staying.'

'No, not at all.' Carey stood and escorted Tedric to the door. 'But you will return. Dine with me later. You can't imagine how insufferably dull this place has been for me. There's nothing but riffraff here.'

Under any other circumstances, Tedric knew, Carey would have regarded him as riffraff, too. 'May my companions join us? I'm afraid, during the course of the time we've spent together, they've come to depend upon me somewhat.'

'Does that include Milton Dass?' Carey said with interest.

It does if he's willing to come and Fra Villion hasn't already grabbed him and put him to work someplace.'

'Villion hasn't been around for days. I'm expecting him shortly, however.' Carey glanced meaningfully around the big room, as if expecting Villion to put in an immediate appearance. 'But don't bring the Wykzl. I'm afraid I can't stand the sight of them.'

'Ky-shan is used to that reaction. He has his own food to eat.'

'Then I'll see you shortly.'

'It will be a pleasure,' said Tedric. He saluted, half seriously, half mockingly.

Carey returned the gesture with a distant look in his eyes. He seemed to be seeing other things, thinking far away thoughts.

Tedric turned and followed Galton along the clean, well-lighted corridor.

CHAPTER 11

Fra Villion Speaks

As the days aboard the Iron Sphere stretched into weeks and those, in turn, approached a full month, Tedric still found more than enough things of interest to fill his waking hours. He saw a great deal of Matthew Carey, a considerable amount of Yod, and Juvi, very little of Milton Dass, and nothing at all of Fra Villion. During the course of their frequent dinner dates, Carey continued to insist that Villion would be appearing soon, but when Tedric pressed to find out how he knew, Carey grew silent, just smiled, and insisted that he understood the tenor of Villion's mind. 'You have to remember that I've known him a lot longer than any other man alive.'

Tedric couldn't understand that claim. Matthew Carey had still been on Earth when Fra Villion had first appeared from the red cloud. Carey refused to elucidate, however, and Tedric couldn't very well disagree without exposing the fact that he knew a great deal more about Villion than he rightly should.

The rank of commander excused him from regular duty. Most of his time was therefore occupied familiarising himself with the geography of the Iron Sphere. It was a fascinating construct – a genuine alien relic. If nothing else, the sophistication and complexity of the Sphere quite convinced Tedric of Fra Villion's identity as a Bioman. The Sphere simply did not belong in the Empire of Man.

The core of the Sphere, a good fifth of its total volume, was given over to the circuitry and machines that kept the artificial planetoid functioning. Tedric had managed to invade these forbidden precincts on a number of occasions. Though guards were posted at all entrances he had slipped past them, but in the event had learned nothing useful. It was like an electronic madhouse down there. Perhaps Milton Dass might have begun to comprehend a portion of the innards, but Tedric was not Dass, and his knowledge failed to encompass a single thing that he saw.

Somewhere above the core were the inhabited decks. Even then, the size of the Sphere was greater than the needs of its crew, and the bulk of the deck space went unused. Every man aboard had been assigned a private room, and while none were as large as Matthew Carey's, all were bigger than the average stateroom on an interstellar liner. There was also a large recreation facility, including a gymnasium, ballroom, and a vast tridee bank. Tedric counted four automatic kitchens, two largely unused libraries, and more than twenty bars dispensing every variety of intoxicant imaginable.

None of this meant however, that the crew was pampered. On the contrary, duty assignments were rigidly enforced. The majority of these consisted of labour in the ship construction facilities. All the necessary parts and components for creating a large space fleet had come with the Sphere, but it was now necessary to take those parts and put them together. Every day either Yod or Juvi – sometimes both – worked twelve to fourteen hours at this. On many occasions, Tedric went up to observe. What he saw both fascinated and worried him. The ships were obviously of alien design. Only their engines – the basic N-space drive – resembled imperial models. And he observed them being tested, too, wandering up to the docking facilities in the top deck. The ships were fast, efficient, and capable of quick, neat manoeuvring. All were thoroughly well-armed, with shields, tractor beams, and a variety of heat-ray weapons. The imperial fleet would have a difficult time resisting any attack in force by such ships. And that wasn't even considering the power inherent in the Sphere itself – or Dass's matter-scrambler.

Like Tedric, Milton Dass had been appointed a commander and excused from regular duty. Unlike Tedric, Dass seemed unable to find enough distractions to fill his days. Whenever he wanted him, Tedric could invariably find Dass either sitting alone in his own room or else in the recreational facility, where he sat off by himself, watching tridee and consuming a variety of rich foods. He seemed morose, distracted, indifferent, and sullen. There were times when he hardly seemed to recognise Tedric or know his own name. 'I never used to eat anything,' he told Tedric one day, patting his blossoming stomach. 'It was the only way I could think. When I built the matter-scrambler, I starved myself for nine days beforehand.'

With anyone else, Tedric would have interpreted this as a gross exaggeration, but Dass never exaggerated. 'I hope it was worth it.'

'Worth what?' asked Dass.

'The hunger. What about your wife? I thought she was supposed to be here. Haven't you seen her yet?'

'Oh, I've seen her, all right. She's here.' He was trying too hard to be casual.

'Then why isn't she with you?' Tedric said, indicating the room where both men stood. Dass kept his personal area so scrupuously clean and neat that it was difficult to tell that anyone lived here.

'Oh, they've put her to work. You know, like Yod and Juvi, a regular duty shift. You and I are commanders and thus excused, but she's just a common soldier – or sailor.'

Tedric nodded his head politely, but he didn't believe a word Dass was telling him. The good thing about Dass's penchant for telling the truth was that, when he was forced to lie, he did it poorly. 'How did you manage to find your wife? You told me Villion had taken her prisoner. Was she released as soon as we arrived or did you have to go and search for her?'

'Oh, she came to me.'

'I thought she was a prisoner.'

'Well, aren't we all? Here, I mean. There's no way out, is there?'

Tedric had to agree that that was true enough, and yet Dass's evasiveness concerning the present fate of his wife continued to puzzle him.

He decided to question Matthew Carey to see what, if anything, he knew. Carey readily admitted that he had known Lola Dass for many years. Both had attended the imperial school on Earth at the same time. Her family possessed a long and glorious heritage but they were far from wealthy. Dass's family was exactly the opposite. He was himself a very rich man, thanks to a number of practical inventions devised early in his career.

'A marriage between them was thus a convenience for everyone,' Carey said. 'That's not unusual, but I still can't think of a more bizarre coupling.'

'Because of the disparity in their ages?'

'Partially, yes, but that's not unusual, either. What I'm talking about is the fact that at the time of their marriage Dass was living in an insane asylum.'

Tedric frowned. 'Dass? He's a little weird, but I'd not have thought him insane.'

'He's supposed to be a genius. I don't know about that, but I do know he'd completely lost his mind a few years ago. That's what made the marriage so appealing for Lola. She could have a rich husband without ever having to set eyes on him.'

'Something must have happened.'

'It did. Dass recovered. During the marriage ceremony itself, if legend is to be believed. I wish I could have been there to see her face. It must have been fantastic.'

'Dass seems to love her very much.'

'Wouldn't you? He thinks she cured him, made him sane again.'

'That's why he went to work for Fra Villion.'

'Oh?' Carey seemed very interested. 'Did he tell you that?'

'He told me Fra Villion kidnapped his wife and forced him to work for him.'

'Oh, that. Yes, I suppose that's true enough.'

'And she's here now?'

'Lola? Oh yes.'

'Where?'

Carey's suspicion showed plainly. 'Why do you want to know?'

'I'm just curious. Dass claims to love her so much and yet they're still not together. Did Fra Villion refuse to fulfil his part of the bargain? If Villion can't be trusted, it would be worthwhile for me to know it.'

Carey could well understand that sort of cool calculation. 'I'll tell you this much. Villion was not the one who decided.'

'Decided what?'

'Where Lola Dass wants to stay.'

Tedric still wasn't sure that he fully understood, but there was nothing to be gained by pressing the point too far and arousing Carey's barely suppressed suspicions once more. He let the matter drop.

A few days later, Fra Villion finally materialised in the flesh. Tedric sat in moody silence in his own room, a victim at last of imposed idleness, when the viewscreen on the wall flickered unexpectedly to life and showed the solemn face of Matthew Carey. His message, when he spoke, was brief and cautious. 'All crew members are hereby directed to report at once to the central auditorium to receive further orders from your commander-in-chief, Fra Villion.' Even though Tedric had shared dinner with Carey just a few hours before, Carey had given no hint of this development. Either Carey was very expert at concealing secrets or else Fra Villion made it a practice to keep his intentions to himself as long as possible.

As the screen went blank again, he turned to Ky-shan. 'What do you think? Is this it?' He found himself unable to prevent a certain amount of eager anticipation from entering his voice.

Ky-shan nodded thoughtfully. The gesture was one he had picked up during his time in the human sphere, and it always struck Tedric as slightly absurd, coming from that oversized alien head. 'I understand that nearly all the ships under construction are close to operational now.'

'Then Villion must be ready to do something.'

'The question is what?' said Ky-shan.

Tedric shook his head. Strapping on his heatgun, he headed for the door. 'Maybe we'd better go and see.'

Outside, the corridor was crowded with men, women, and submen heading for the elevators that led to the auditorium below. Tedric fell into step with the others. Ky-shan, moving behind, loomed over the crowd like a signal flag. Tedric felt an anxious tension spreading through his belly. This was more like it. The last month, even though he had managed to keep himself occupied by surveying the Iron Sphere, had still been an ordeal. He was gratified to be back in action again. He suddenly realised that what the Scientists wanted him to do did not greatly matter in his life. He was simply not a man who could accept idleness gladly. Dropped down in this universe with neither assistance nor direction, he would nevertheless have sought out the nearest conflict and joined one side or the other. For his life to possess meaning required the existence of a definite goal, an end to be reached and achieved. What that goal might be – how real or desired – was less important than the fact that it existed at all. At the moment, his goal was simply to destroy Fra Villion. Once that was accomplished – and he never doubted that eventually it would be – then he would seek out something else to pursue. Perhaps Skandos had told the truth. The Scientists had brought him to this universe because of who he was, not what he would do.

The huge cavern of the central auditorium was already filled with several hundred individuals awaiting the appearance of their commander-in-chief. Tedric stood at the rear of the crowd within easy viewing distance of the raised platform at the centre of the room. The platform was empty at the moment, and the crowd milled restlessly. Spotting Yod and Juvi in a nearby cluster, Tedric edged towards them motioning Ky-shan to follow. Well practiced in the art of surreptitious movement, Tedric crept up behind Yod and, in a swift motion removed the heatgun from his holster.

Yod spun angrily around but when he saw Tedric he lowered his hands. 'What did you do that for?'

Tedric tucked the heatgun into his belt. 'I loaned it to you. I decided I wanted it back.'

Juvi made no effort to conceal her relief. 'Can you believe this idiot?' She jerked her head towards Yod, but kept her voice soft. 'He still wants to get a shot at Villion.'

'He dared me to come here,' Yod said; his determination showed in the anger and tension in his face. 'You heard him yourself.'

'Aren't the odds rather against you?' Tedric said, indicating the crowd around them.

'I don't care about them. It's Villion I'm after.'

'And it's you they'll get if you try something that stupid.'

'I can borrow a gun from someone else.'

Tedric shook his head slowly. 'No, you can't.'

'Are you going to stop me.'

'Yes. I happen to be interested in finding out what Villion intends to say. After he's finished, maybe I'll return your gun.'

'I doubt that. It wasn't your parents he murdered.' Yod turned away from Tedric and stared sullenly at the still deserted platform.

'I think he's crazy,' Juvi said.

'No, just determined.' Tedric sympathised with Yod, but he saw no reason to let the boy kill himself for no good end. Later on, there might be another, better chance, and if that happened, Tedric was more than willing to give Yod first crack at Villion.

There was a sudden muting of the noise in the room, and Tedric turned his head towards the platform. A thin figure was ascending the stairs. It wasn't Villion. It was Matthew Carey.

He seemed ill-at-ease, uncertain of the reception he would receive from the crowd of outlaws gathered here. 'Crew-members,' he cried, his voice spreading hollowly through the auditorium. 'Most of you have only recently joined us here aboard the Iron Sphere and have not yet had the privilege of meeting our leader. It is my supreme pleasure, therefore, to introduce the commander-in-chief of our forces, Fra Villion.'

Carey stepped back, his nervousness still apparent in the stiff way he moved; for a moment, nothing happened. Carey's appearance had created little stir among the crowd. Former Emperor or not, probably fewer than a dozen occupants of the room recognised him for who he was. Renegades and pirates living at the edge of the realm were not likely to follow the political vicissitudes of an empire to which they felt only nominal allegiance at best.

They did know Villion, though, or at least they recognised his importance.

And now at last he was appearing before them in the flesh.

Two figures were materialising on the platform a few steps in front of where Carey stood. One of these was a woman, the other a darkly furred beast. Tedric recognised Fra Villion instantly. And it really was him this time – not just a projected image. Tedric was certain of that. Villion exuded a sense of malevolent, energetic life that was overwhelming in its intensity.

Both figures had materialised out of thin air.

Tedric had no idea how Villion had managed the trick this time. Was it genuine teleportation? Could this be another Bio-man talent?

For a long moment, Villion and his female companion stood motionless on the platform. The room was totally silent. Somewhere, then, a door opened.

Tedric turned his head. Another man had just entered the room. It was Milton Dass. He stood frozen in the doorway, his face a contorted mask of pain and inner anguish. Dass, too, was staring at the platform.

Tedric looked back in spite of himself. Villion wore a black uniform with white collar. A dark cape fell from his shoulders, and a hood covered the top of his skull. He wasn't quite as tall or broad as his projected image but cast an imposing figure nonetheless. The bright hues of his bare face shone under the harsh artificial lights overhead.

The woman was also very tall, although the top of her head barely reached Villion's jaw. Her hair was pure blonde, long and beautiful; her skin was so pale that she might have been carved from ice. She dressed all in black, the same as Villion, but her head was uncovered and the tunic she wore barely reached the top of her bare thighs. Tedric did not think he had ever seen a more striking woman in his life.

Her grey eyes sparkled as she regarded the throng gathered in the auditorium; her face betrayed not the slightest quivering of emotion as, briefly, she glanced at each and every man and woman standing before her.

Villion spoke: 'My servants, I am pleased at last to greet you and discuss the plans I have made for all of us. Before I do so, however, I must introduce my second-in-command.'

Tedric assumed he meant Carey, but Villion pointed at the woman instead. 'This is Lady Lola Dass.'

Tedric straightened in surprise. He looked over his shoulder again, but Dass was no longer in the doorway. He must have guessed the truth, Tedric realised, but somehow had never known for sure until just now. Villion might have kidnapped Lola Dass to begin with, but she was clearly here with him willingly now. If Dass had been prevented from seeing Lola before, as Tedric guessed, he thought it was doubly cruel to force him to learn the truth in this fashion.

Villion went on. 'Any orders from Lady Lola are to be regarded as orders from me. The penalty for disobedience will be instant death.'

He could have told his audience that he wished each one of them to turn and kill his nearest neighbour and ninety per cent would have obeyed. The atmosphere in the room was tense not just with expectancy, but with fear, raw fear.

'Until now,' said Villion, 'I have said nothing of my ultimate intentions. Those of you who have served me longest have participated in numerous expeditionary raids. Others of you, only recently arrived, have perhaps done little but build ships. To all of you, I now address myself. You are a proud assemblage. Never in the history of man has such a collection of criminals, pirates, renegades, and cutthroats been banded together at any one time.'

A few people could be heard laughing appreciatively, but they soon fell silent. Lightness was clearly not the mood of the moment.

'The time has now come to proceed forward. In a few hours time, I will issue the order that will send the Iron Sphere into the realm of N-space. We are well equipped and supplied. A weapon has come into my possession that will render all resistance futile, a weapon capable of destroying a planet. My servants, I am pleased to announce that our objective is the destruction of Earth.'

Tedric nodded softly, amazed by his own lack of surprise. What Villion had just announced seemed so obvious that he felt irritated by his failure to guess the truth from the beginning.

The pirate raids had served largely as camouflage. Villion's ultimate goal must have been clear in his mind from the moment he had entered the Empire. Tedric could easily guess Villion's motive in destroying Earth, but reasons were of little importance; Villion had to be stopped – that was all that mattered now.

'Once the Earth is destroyed,' Villion said, the coolness of his voice failing to disguise the horror of his message, 'nothing can possibly stand in our path. The Empire of Man will belong to us and us alone. I believe I can guarantee that each of you will share equally in the rewards soon to fall upon us.'

This last statement was greeted by applause and some cheers, but the reponse was far from overwhelming. Villion had been extremely general in his guarantees and apparently at least some of his audience had noticed that. Then, too, many of the men and women must have had friends and even relatives living on the Earth. The destruction of the greatest planet in the Empire would not necessarily please even a band of renegade outlaws. A raid, even conquest, yes, perhaps – but destruction was different; destruction was permanent.

Villion, too, seemed to sense this uncertainty. He stood rigidly, eyes raking the motley crowd beneath him with a fierce glare. 'Are there any questions?' he drawled. 'Or, perhaps, some objections?'

Tedric could feel the restiveness of the crowd. If one person spoke out, others would surely follow, but Villion's gaze was almost hypnotic in its intensity. Tedric could see people's lips moving, but no actual words emerged. Villion held them firmly in his grasp. Above all else, he had already taught them to fear him.

'Good,' said Villion, relaxing suddenly. Reaching over, he gripped the hand of his companion and pressed it firmly. 'In that case, expect to receive more specific directions through the established chain of command. Until future events bring us together again, I bid you good-bye. Group, dismissed.'

Villion vanished. An instant later, Lola Dass followed him. Tedric stared open-mouthed at the platform, now deserted except for the forlorn figure of Matthew Carey. Even though he understood the probable origin of Villion's powers, he could not avoid experiencing a shiver of primordial fear and awe.

All at once, the auditorium erupted with the tumult of several hundred voices speaking simultaneously. Yod Cartwright turned towards Tedric. 'Did you hear that?' he said, his voice choked with emotion. 'He intends to destroy the Earth! Destroy the Earth after all he's already done.'

Tedric couldn't afford to seem too sympathetic. It was always possible, even in this cacophony, that someone might be listening. 'I heard what he said.'

'And what are we going to do about it?' Yod cried.

Tedric shook his head. He spoke with deliberate ambiguity. 'I don't know that there's a great deal we can do.'

'I can think of at least one thing,' Yod said heatedly.

Juvi intervened quickly, changing the subject before Yod could say something else foolish. 'Who was that woman with Fra Villion? I don't think I've seen her before.'

'That was Dass's wife,' Tedric said.

Juvi didn't seem to know whether to laugh or cry. 'I heard him say the name but I never thought . . . Dass's wife! Poor Milton.'

Tedric shook his head, suddenly distracted. He did not feel much in the mood for idle chatter. Villion's threat still stood uppermost in his mind, and he knew he must act promptly if he wanted to thwart him. But how? His options were surely limited. He needed time alone in which to think.

Turning sharply on his heel, he headed for the door.

A voice called after him. 'Tedric, hold on.'

It was Yod. Tedric stopped.

'Yod held out his hand. 'Won't you give me back my gun?'

Tedric started to shake his head negatively, then reconsidered. 'I'll do it on one condition. I want your word you'll keep it in your holster.'

'If I promise that, then I don't need the gun.'

'Not now,' Tedric said meaningfully, 'but, perhaps, later. Be patient and you may get a chance to use it.'

Yod looked hard at Tedric. 'What do you mean by that?'

'I mean just what I said.'

'You aren't a renegade, are you? You're still a corpsman. I'll bet – '

Tedric held out the gun. 'Don't confuse a corpsman's bearing with a corpsman's loyalty. Give me your word and take the gun.'

Yod still hesitated. At last, his shoulders drooped. 'All right, I promise, but – '

'Take the gun.'

Yod took the weapon and pushed it into his holster. 'Then I'll see you later,' he said softly.

'I hope so.'

Yod nodded, turned away, and went back to Juvi.

Ky-shan placed his hand on Tedric's shoulder. 'He is a very excitable young man,' he said.

'And he has a big mouth,' said Tedric quietly.

Tedric hurried on towards the door. There was a crowd milling in front of it, some trying to leave, others just talking, but Tedric had little difficulty making his exit. He wasn't Fra Villion but he cut an imposing figure nonetheless. The way people hurried to get out of his path made him grin wryly. Do I look that determined? he wondered. That mean? He only hoped, when the time came for a showdown, that Fra Villion would feel similarly intimidated. He doubted that would happen, though. Fra Villion wasn't just an outlaw. He was a Bioman *vemplar* and surely the most powerful opponent Tedric had ever faced in his life.

CHAPTER 12

The Black Knight

Turning away from the blank white wall, Tedric sat up on his bunk and faced the room for the first time in several hours. Ky-shan, who had been waiting patiently, gave no outward indication of any sense of relief that this tedious ordeal of waiting might finally be over.

'I want you to go get Yod Cartwright,' Tedric said.

'And bring him here?'

'Yes. At once, please.'

Ky-shan headed obediently towards the door.

'And tell him to be sure to bring his heatgun,' Tedric added.

The Wykzl paused with one big hand on the doorknob. 'Then you have found him?'

'I believe so. If I'm wrong, we'll have to try again.'

'And if he is there?'

'Then we'll have to try to kill him.'

Ky-shan nodded gently. 'I believe that is the wisest course to follow, Tedric.'

It was rare for Ky-shan to offer his opinion concerning anything, and Tedric appreciated the fact that he had done so now. It helped to alleviate any remaining doubts that Tedric himself might possess. 'I thank you for telling me that, Ky-shan.'

'You are welcome, Tedric.' Ky-shan went out.

Tedric lay down and turned his face back to the wall. Once again, he carefully reviewed the logic that had guided him towards his present course, and once again that logic seemed quite unassailable. He knew exactly where he could find Fra Villion, and he knew exactly what he must do when he got there. Still, he could be wrong. Nothing was that certain. Normally, he would have proceeded in spite of this, but the present situation was different. If he failed, if Villion survived, then absolutely nothing would stand between him and the ultimate destruction of Earth.

The first action Tedric had taken after leaving the meeting in the auditorium was to visit the docks on the topmost level of the Sphere. He went alone since Ky-shan's presence tended to disturb people unduly. The captain of the watch, a squat, dark-skinned man named Bik, recognised Tedric's rank and offered a precise salute.

Tedric returned the gesture casually. He spoke in a soothing, friendly undertone. 'I was wondering if it was possible to get a look at that ship.'

'Ship? Which ship, sir?' Bik seemed genuinely puzzled. He wasn't an ordinary pirate. Tedric knew the man by name. A former cadet at the Academy, Bik had been kicked out for cheating in an examination. Apparently some of his military training had taken effect. He continued to stand stiffly at attention.

Tedric laid a confidential hand on his shoulder. 'You know the one I mean. Fra Villion's ship. I heard it was quite a thing to see and I'd like to take a look at it.'

'Fra Villion? But he has no ship.'

'He just arrived here, didn't he?'

'No, sir. Not during my watch.'

'Then the one before.'

'The only ship presently in the docks is a raiding vessel only just returned from the Abralian Sector. It's been here several hours now.'

Tedric was willing to take Bik at his word. He doubted if the man had the imagination to carry through a good lie. 'Then I guess someone steered me wrong. I'm interested in ships – you used to belong to the Corps, so you'll understand – and someone told me that Fra Villion's was here.'

'They were wrong, sir. I've seen Fra Villion only the once in my life. At the meeting just now. As far as I know, he's been here all along.'

'Then isn't it odd that no one's ever seen him before?'

Bik shrugged. He seemed totally uncurious about the course

of events. 'They say he can move through air without the benefit of any conveyance.'

Tedric went away. The chance remained, assuming that Bik indeed spoke the truth, that Villion had arrived during another watch, but Tedric understood the innate tendency of all men to gossip. Something as dramatic as the arrival of Fra Villion would not remain a secret for long. Villion had never arrived at the docks – not recently at least. Bik was right: Villion had been aboard the Sphere all this time. But where? That was the question Tedric needed to answer. Wherever Villion had hidden before was undoubtedly where he could be found this moment. And Tedric wanted to find him. As soon as possible.

He returned to his room, lay down on his bunk, and began to consider. In the past month, he had surveyed the Sphere from top level to bottom. He mentally reviewed everything he had discovered. There were only two major question marks. One was the huge area in the centre of the Sphere where the various engines, computers, and other gadgetry were located. He had explored only a tiny portion of those decks, and it was quite conceivable that Villion might be living somewhere down there. Conceivable, yes – likely, no. Tedric had seen enough of the core of the Sphere to guess what the rest of it must be like: hot, noisy, uncomfortable, unpleasant. For the sake of his own isolation, Villion might personally be willing to endure such conditions, but only if he was alone. What about Lola Dass? How long had she been with Villion? Tedric had seen the vast, ornate domicile she had occupied on Nykzas. Would she willingly accept much less here on the Iron Sphere? She would, of course, if she was actually a prisoner, but from what Tedric had seen today, a prisoner she certainly was not.

Tedric remembered the look on Dass's face in the auditorium. He sensed that it wouldn't hurt to talk to him before proceeding further. He had sent Ky-shan to fetch him.

Nearly a half-hour passed before the Wykzl returned. When he did, he was alone.

'Couldn't you find him?' Tedric asked.

'I – I – yes and no.' Ky-shan seemed peculiarly flustered. 'Milton Dass has been placed under arrest, Tedric. He went mad – beserk – in the upper levels and caused extensive damage. It took a half-dozen men to subdue him.'

'Did you go to see yourself?'

'I tried as soon as I heard, but I arrived too late. He was already gone.'

'You didn't see Villion there?'

'No, Tedric.'

He nodded Dass's arrest was something else to ponder. Tedric did so, sifting that and everything else he had so far discovered. In the end one definite conclusion seemed inescapable. He was certain he knew where Villion was hiding. It wasn't in the core of the Sphere – he eliminated that possibility – it was in the one other place he had never been able to inspect firsthand. Immediately next to Matthew Carey's quarters lay a closed set of rooms, the corridor doors firmly locked. Making use of a tool he had once acquired from an acquaintance who earned a good living burgling New Melbourne's finest homes, he had broken the locks, but the doors remained barred. That was a puzzle. If the rooms were unoccupied, how had the doors come to be blocked from the inside? He had once attempted to question Carey as casually as possible concerning the matter.

Carey had looked at him blankly. 'As far as I know, no one lives there. It's a general storage area.'

'Have you been inside to see?'

Carey couldn't hide the suspicion that suddenly washed through him, evidence in itself that the situation wasn't quite as harmless as he wanted to make it seem. 'Why should I? It's nothing but old boxes and crates.'

Tedric did not try to push the matter further at that time, but his curiosity had definitely been aroused and now, through the process of elimination if nothing else, he was convinced. Villion had plainly kept in touch with Carey these past few weeks. What better way than to have the rooms right next to his?

Once his mind was firmly made up – and not until that moment – Tedric turned to Ky-shan and ordered him to fetch Yod Cartwright.

Yod seemed hesitant and uncertain as he entered the room accompanied by the giant Wykzl. Once the door was safely closed and locked, Tedric sat up straight and spoke directly. 'I made a promise of sorts to you and I intend to keep it. I've decided to make an attempt on the life of Fra Villion. You're welcome to come along if you wish.'

Yod made no effort to conceal his pleasure. 'But I thought you were – '

'Never mind who or what I am. You can either trust me or not. If you want to come, I'll expect you to obey my commands to the letter. If you'd rather return to your room, I'd appreciate your saying nothing of this conversation for the time being.'

Yod continued to gape. 'Then you are serious.'

'Totally.'

'Then I – then of course I'll go with you. I want to kill him as much as you – more than you.'

Tedric shook his head wearily. 'This isn't a child's game, Yod. Villion won't laugh and set you free this time. If we fail, we'll both die.'

Yod drew himself stiffly upright. 'I'm not afraid.'

'Well, I am,' said Tedric. 'And you should be, too, if you've got half a brain in your head. Fra Villion is a very powerful individual. Exactly how powerful I won't know until I've faced him.'

'Then let's go.' His face as stern as an iron mask, Yod turned towards the door.

Tedric couldn't help laughing. 'Hold on a minute. There's not that much rush. You brought your gun? Good. Now what about Juvi? Does she know you're here?'

'She was in the room when Ky-shan came. I suppose she must.'

Tedric shrugged. 'It probably doesn't matter. If we succeed and Villion dies, then everyone will know what we've done soon enough. If we fail, then we'll be dead, and damn little will matter then.'

'I'm aware of the risk.'

'Good. That's what I want to hear from you. Awareness, not blind courage.'

Standing, Tedric pulled his heatgun out of its holster and carefully examined the charge. He asked Yod for his gun and checked it, too.

That accomplished, he waved a hand at the door. 'Shall we go?'

The three of them went. The corridor was emptier than usual – new duty assignments had already been instituted in preparation for the journey into N-space – and their passage aroused no curious glances from the few people they did meet. They were simply two men and an alien going about their usual business. At one point, Yod tried to ask a question about their ultimate destination, but Tedric cut him short. He wanted his mind free from all distractions. He wanted to concentrate strictly on the problems that lay ahead. One incorrect manoeuvre, a single slip or stumble, might well mean his own death. He tried to concentrate on how easy this was going to be. He knew where Villion was. He would go there, force his way inside, and kill him before he could raise a hand.

It sounded easy enough. In actuality, he knew it wouldn't be.

His entire plan of attack would have failed if Matthew Carey had decided not to be home. Fortunately, only moments after Tedric knocked, the door swung open and Carey stood staring at him in surprise.

Keeping the heatgun concealed by the bulk of his body, Tedric pushed the barrel snugly against Carey's chest. 'Inside,' he whispered. 'And quickly.'

Carey made no objection, backing gingerly into the room. Yod and Ky-shan slipped through the half-open door. When they were safely inside, Tedric kicked it shut with the back of his foot, never taking his eyes from Carey.

'What do you want?' Carey said. He spoke softly, careful not to rile the man with the gun. 'Have you lost your mind, too, like Dass?'

Tedric suppressed a grin. Considering the boldness of what he was contemplating, Carey's accusation wasn't that far from the mark. 'I want you to show me the way in there,' he said, jerking his head towards the wall.

Carey started to reply, but stopped. His mouth kept working like a fish removed from the water. Finally, he managed to speak. 'In there? What for? There's nothing in there.'

'I want to find out for myself.'

'You *are* crazy.'

'I only want to talk to Fra Villion.'

'He's not in there.' Carey spoke quickly – too quickly – and seemed to realise the error himself. Back-pedalling deeper into the room, he held his hands out in front of him. 'We trusted you. After you destroyed Milrod Eleven, how could we doubt your loyalty?'

Tedric saw no reason to tell Carey the truth about the destruction of that world. There was a good chance that he, Tedric, would not live another hour, in which case, with Fra Villion the dominant force in the Empire, it was best that Carey continue to believe in the fact of his sister's death. 'You miscalculated,' he said.

'But why reveal your hand now? Villion will simply kill you, squash you like a pest.'

'I intend to kill him first.'

Carey laughed hollowly, but Tedric noticed that he was no longer denying that Villion lived next door. 'You can't be serious. You've seen Villion. He's more powerful than any of us can imagine. I've worked with him for a long time, Tedric. He's much more than human.'

Tedric realised that Carey wasn't simply trying to distract him. The man had probably never spoken more sincerely in his life. 'No living thing has yet been created that cannot die.'

'Villion may be the first.'

'I intend to find out.'

Carey came forward. 'I like you, Tedric. I always have, ever since we were both junior cadets at the Academy. You've got brains and nerve and courage. Leave Villion alone. Go back to your room and stay there and I promise never to say a word about this to anyone. Who knows? Maybe someday Villion will go back where he came from and the Empire will belong to us again.'

'Belong to you, is what you mean.'

Carey shook his head. 'Somehow being Emperor doesn't seem very important anymore. I've lost control. He killed my father and my sister and I suppose when I've shed whatever usefulness I might still possess he'll kill me, too.'

Then you ought to help me kill him if you really feel that way.'

'I wish I could. I wish there was a way. There isn't. Go back to your room, Tedric, and admit that Fra Villion is too powerful for any mere human.'

'I can't let him destroy Earth.'

'Earth?' Carey laughed bitterly. 'What do you care about Earth? It's not your home.'

Tedric looked at Carey narrowly. 'What do you mean by that?'

'I mean that you were born in another universe and brought here against your will. You're a puppet, the same as I am – worse than I am.'

'Who told you that?'

'Who do you think?' He jerked his head at the wall. 'He did. He knows everything.'

Tedric bit his lip thoughtfully, genuinely dismayed for the first time. How could Fra Villion know that much about him? He felt despair welling up and battled against it. He sensed their presence, those adversaries against whom the Scientists warred. Not Fra Villion himself perhaps, but just beyond him – and very close.

Tedric pointed at the wall. 'Open it. I know there's a door. We're going through.'

With a heavy sigh, Carey moved to obey. 'Don't say I didn't warn you.'

Under Tedric's watchful eye, Carey crossed the room, placed his hand against an apparently blank spot on the wall, and stood back as a door slid open. Tedric couldn't help thinking of a creaky, old-fashioned tridee melodrama. Carey had revealed a secret passage linking the two rooms. Beyond the door, it was dark.

Tedric pointed with his gun. 'Go through first.'

'Me?' Carey stood rigidly. 'This is your business, not mine.'

'You can go through dead or alive. It's your choice.'

Carey still didn't move. 'Then it'll have to be dead. If Fra Villion sees me with you, he won't ask questions. I'd just as soon die now as then.'

From the glint of confident amusement in Carey's eyes, it was clear that he did not expect Tedric to kill him.

'I'll tell you what I'll do,' Tedric said. 'As you know, a heat-gun is not only capable of killing, it can burn. I'm going to adjust the setting. I'll start at the lowest, weakest level and move progressively higher. At first it'll feel like a sunburn. Then it'll get hotter. Your skin will crisp and char. The flesh will burn. I may not want to kill you, Matthew, but I don't mind roasting you alive.' Reaching down with a thumb, Tedric flicked the tiny dial set in the butt of the weapon. He kept the barrel aimed steadily. 'Are you ready?'

Carey looked impressed. 'I do believe you'd do it.'

'Want to test me?'

'Not especially.' He stepped towards the wall. 'All right. Let's go.'

Tedric went after him. He gestured to Yod and Ky-shan to follow.

The room on the opposite side of the secret door was pitch dark. Tedric clutched the tail of Carey's jacket and held him fast until enough time had passed for his eyes to adjust to the dark. He could always see better under such conditions than anyone else he knew. The talent might have originated in the special light of the world into which he had first been born. He remembered that universe as a grey and misty place. What he saw now was a large empty room.

He whispered, 'Where now?'

'Through the door,' said Carey pointing at the opposite wall.

'Will Villion be there?'

'It's possible, but I doubt it. The next room is hers.'

'Whose?'

'Lola's. I thought you knew. She always was a sly one. She's hitched her fate to a rising star.'

'How long has she been here?'

'Longer than I have.'

'Go. And not a word. I won't kill you unless I have to, but if you cross me, I won't hesitate.'

Carey crossed the room on silent feet. He placed his palm against the wall and another door slid open. Tedric shut his eyes to avoid being blinded by the sudden flood of bright light.

When he opened them, Carey still stood in the arch of the door. He waved an impatient hand. Tedric went to him.

This second room was slightly larger than the first, but there was really no comparison. It might have been the private bedroom of a princess in a palace: a huge canopied bed, ornately carved wooden dresser, a carpet three inches thick.

'Fra Villion wanted to make her feel at home,' Carey said.

Tedric looked across the room to the opposite wall. 'There's another room beyond?'

'Three more, I believe.'

'Where do you usually find Villion?'

'In the next one or the one after that.'

'What's the next room?'

'His private armoury.'

'What?'

'That's what I call it. Villion collects weapons. He likes to practice.'

'Then you go through alone. Keep the door open. If he's there, talk to him. Distract him if you can.'

'He won't be happy. He's not accustomed to having me drop in uninvited.'

'I'm sure you can think of something to say. Now go.' Tedric waved his gun.

Carey stepped forward. Tedric, Yod, and Ky-shan followed cautiously. Carey pointed to the place in the wall where the door ought to be. Tedric placed himself and Yod on one side of the opening and sent Ky-shan over to the other. At a nod from Tedric, Carey placed his palm against the wall. The door slid open. If Carey saw anything beyond, he gave no immediate indication. He stepped through. Tedric tensed himself to spring. If the door slammed shut, he intended to leap through.

For a long moment, there was silence. Tedric cocked his ears to pick up any stray noises. All he heard was Yod Cartwright's tense breathing at his shoulder.

Then, suddenly, from beyond the open door, a voice spoke. It was by now familiar, Fra Villion. 'What are you doing here, Carey?'

Tedric could visualise Carey's casual shrug. 'I just wanted to discuss your little speech, Fra.'

'And what concern is that of yours?'

'Well, the Earth did used to be my home.'

'You want me to reconsider my strategy?'

'I think you ought to think about what you're doing.'

Carey was playing his role well – perhaps too well Tedric had anticipated at least one attempt at trickery, and the fact that Carey had tried nothing disturbed him. He was tempted to peek through the open door to confirm the existence of the scene his ears told him was being played out, but he held back. If Villion really was present – and he had no legitimate reason for suspecting that he was not – it was wiser to let Carey continue to lull him before making a move.

Villion said, 'You are free to elaborate your opinions.'

Carey did so, droning on. He talked about how easy it would be to bring the Empire to its knees by the simple act of destroying an outlying planet. 'Show them the strength we possess and they'll throw up their hands. I know men better than you do, Villion. After all, I'm one of them myself.'

'We have destroyed a planet, Milrod Eleven, and there has been no surrender.'

'That's because nobody knows how it happened. Once they've seen the Iron Sphere, they'll realise the hopelessness of further resistance.'

Tedric sensed that it was time to act. Moving cautiously, he stepped into the door space, heatgun levelled. He could see Carey clearly in the middle of the room. He was standing, talking, waving his arms excitedly. But where was Fra Villion? Tedric could hear his voice plainly, but its direction was difficult to gauge. He had to lean into the room in order to see every corner. He did so, but Villion was not present. Carey was alone in the chamber.

A trick, after all. Well, Tedric couldn't say he was surprised. He was about to step back behind the cover of the wall when Villion interrupted Carey in mid-sentence. 'Ah, Tedric,' said his voice. 'I see you there. Won't you come in and join us?'

Tedric took a step forward. Behind him, Yod and Ky-shan remained concealed in the darkened room.

He could see why Carey had called this place an armoury. There were guns, swords, knives, spears, shields, and clubs stacked everywhere. Many of the weapons were totally unfamiliar to him. Under other conditions, it might have been interesting to examine them.

'You can see me, Fra Villion, but I'm afraid I can't see you.'

Carey was looking at Tedric with a helpless expression on his face, but Tedric didn't believe his innocence for a moment. 'He tricked me,' Carey mouthed, but Tedric didn't believe that, either. Carey was sufficiently clever to wish to remain in good graces with everyone. After all, it was always conceivable that Tedric might yet emerge from this confrontation with not only his life but a victory.

'I must apologise,' said Villion's disembodied voice. 'I'm afraid my shyness sometimes leads me to seem impolite.'

Suddenly, without warning, Villion was there in the room. Lola Dass stood beside him. She smiled at Tedric and her pale eyes seemed to appraise him with more than a little interest. Tedric began to understand why Milton Dass had been driven mad by her loss.

'That's quite a trick, Fra Villion,' he said. 'Can all Biomen manage it?'

Villion showed no surprise at Tedric's knowledge of his identity. 'It requires only a degree of mental discipline. My bride, as you can see, has already been an apt pupil.'

'Your bride?' said Tedric. 'I thought Lady Lola already had one husband.' As he spoke, he made sure his glance met Carey's eyes. He wanted to warn him to say nothing of the presence of Ky-shan and Yod. He hefted the heatgun in his hand. Fra Villion clearly did not fear the weapon, but Carey just might.

'If you refer to Milton Dass, I'm sorry to report that he has left us.'

'You've killed him?' Tedric felt a moment's sorrow. He would miss the poor, sad, brilliant little man.

'I would never kill one who has assisted me so nobly. Milton not only provided me with a wonderful weapon, he also gave me a wonderful woman. But what of you, Tedric? To what do I owe the pleasure of this visit?'

Carey started to answer for him, but Tedric silenced him with a flick of the wrist. There were several ways he could handle this now. It was necessary to extemporise. His eyes took in the entirety of the room. He noticed the piles of various weapons available. 'I've come to challenge you to a duel to the death, Fra Villion.'

Only Lola Dass showed any real surprise. Carey grinned from ear-to-ear, as if a favourite pupil had just proved his mettle, while Villion's expression, as always, was impossible to decipher. 'But why, Tedric? Have I failed to please you?'

'That isn't the question. You are a black knight, a *vemplar*, a great warrior. I merely wish to see for myself if you're as good as you're supposed to be.' He was counting on Fra Villion's vanity to give him a chance. Carelessly, he let the heatgun slip from his grasp and clatter to the floor. 'You can select the weapons of your choice.'

Fra Villion appeared to consider Tedric's offer. Carey's tense expression showed the strain of the moment. At that Villion laughed. 'Then whipswords it will be,' he said.

'And I want the real you, no image. I want someone I can kill.'

'What you see before you now is real enough. Mental projection is a difficult, exhausting art. It's handy only for distant communication.'

There was a strangled cry from behind. Tedric turned in time to see Yod Cartwright burst into the room. He held his heatgun high – too high, Tedric thought, for an accurate shot. Ky-shan lumbered after him, but it was too late to halt Yod's frantic charge.

Tedric saw Yod's finger tighten upon the heatgun's trigger, but never finished the gesture. All at once, he froze as he was. He stood like a statue, one leg raised in the air. Ky-shan, still in dogged pursuit, froze likewise.

'What have you done to them?' Tedric asked Villion.

'Another trick of mine. Nothing permanently harmful. When we're finished, I'll free them again.' He crossed the room in a swirl of black silk and picked two objects off the floor. Both resembled silver sword hilts but without the usual blade. Villion tossed one to Tedric. 'Press the button in the side. The whip will appear.'

Tedric found the button referred to and pressed down with his thumb. The weapon seemed to quiver in his hand, and something shot out of one end. It was a blade as thin as piano wire. Tedric shook his wrist. The blade whipped through the air with a shrill whistling noise. As it moved, the blade was a blur of motion.

'The traditional hand weapon of the *vemplars*,' said Villion. 'Not the most effective but surely the most difficult to master. A thrust is impossible to parry. To succeed in combat, one must learn to move with the grace of a ballerina.'

Tedric waved the whipsword. 'Will it kill?'

'A single slash of the whip blade will sever an arm or leg. Decapitation is the traditional ending for a duel among *vemplars*.'

'Then we'll use the same rules. How about teleportation? Is that allowed?'

'Under sophisticated circumstances, yes. Considering your handicap, I will voluntarily forgo such manoeuvres.'

'Do you really think this is fair? The weapon is totally unfamiliar to me.'

'You issued the original challenge. Besides, I doubt that *Lord* Tedric is unfamiliar with any weapon.'

Tedric smiled narrowly, but in truth his familiarity with the whipsword was very slight. If he was going to die, however, he preferred to go with a weapon clutched in his hand, even this one. He glanced around the room, noting the presence of possible obstructions. Ky-shan and Yod stood mute and frozen. Carey had shifted his position to a safe corner. Lola Dass stood wide-eyed, as if transfixed by the spectacle about to unfold. She wet her lips with the tip of her tongue and glanced nervously at Tedric.

'Then let us proceed.' Villion pushed the button on the side of the handle, and the whip-blade appeared. He turned his wrist delicately to the right and left, testing the feel of the blade, slicing neat chunks out of the air. Finally satisfied, he lowered his arm rigidly and let the sword blade rest against the floor. He murmured a phrase in a language that seemed related to Galactic. The Bioman tongue, Tedric guessed. Fra Villion was quoting an invocation.

As Tedric dropped to a crouch so a series of strange syllables popped into his head and he found himself uttering them aloud.

Another invocation? he wondered. B
what? To those distant gods he had left
his birth? Perhaps, he decided.

'Attack,' said Villion softly. And, without
he lunged forward.

Tedric had to spring back at once as Villion raising,
in an upward sweep. The blade whistled past the tip o
nose. He raised his hand to swing in reply, but Villio
already darted out of range. In spite of his size, Villion mo
without effort. He was more like a dancer than a swordsman.

Again, Villion lunged forward, both feet briefly leaving the floor in a poised leap. Automatically, Tedric raised his weapon to ward off the blow, then remembered what Villion had cautioned him against. To parry would not only be useless, it might well be dangerous. His own blade could only deflect the thrust of Villion's blow, sending the blade whipping out of control. He dropped his hand and ducked his head. The whip-blade passed directly above. Tedric felt the hairs on his skull standing on end.

Lola Dass stood with her fingers on her cheeks. Her face was a mask of excitement; every time a blade passed close to its victim, she screamed. Does she care who wins? Tedric wondered. Or is it only the thrill of the battle that matters?

Villion had stepped out of range again. Tedric thought Villion might well have killed him then, as he stood with his head bowed, but Villion had chosen to withdraw without striking a second blow. He was deliberately extending the length of the match for his own enjoyment. That was an indication of confidence – too much so, Tedric hoped. If he could only take advantage of it. But how?

Tedric moved clumsily to the right, raising his sword. As he did, Villion went with him. Suddenly, Tedric shifted his weight to the other foot. He leapt into the air and swung at the same time. I've got him! he thought triumphantly. He was wrong. Villion tumbled backward. The whip-blade swept past impotently. Villion turned a somersault and landed on his feet. Tedric could only gape. That was an acrobatic manoeuvre he could never hope to duplicate. Then he saw something that made him smile. In the centre of Villion's chest, a red stain of the blade had cut him, after all. who bled could be killed.

s/as clever as you are strong, Tedric,' said Villion. en cut fewer than a dozen times in my service. You ned some illustrious company.'

single cut does not decide a battle, Fra Villion,' Tedric modestly.

'You are an honest man, too.' Villion lumbered forward. For a moment, the sheer awkwardness of his advance caught Tedric by surprise. He expected some sort of feint, a tactic designed to catch him off-guard, but Villion kept coming. Tedric stepped back to avoid the rush and his spine struck hard against the wall. In the excitement of the previous exchange, he had forgotten his position. Villion stopped and swung his arm. Tedric ducked his head, but he knew there was no escape.

This time, Fra Villion moved without mercy. Tedric felt the bite of the whipsword deep in his right shoulder. He chewed his lip to keep from crying out and nearly dropped his own weapon. His whole arm was numb, and he could feel the blood soaking his torn shirt. Quickly, he switched the whipsword to his left hand. He didn't look at the wound.

I give you the option of surrender,' said Villion, stepping back.

Tedric fought to keep the agony from showing in his voice. 'Is that permitted?'

'For one as courageous as you, yes.'

'And then what. Then will you kill me another way?'

'Not if you agree to serve me.'

'I did that once.'

'But this time there are no secrets between us.'

Tedric raised his left arm limply. 'I still have this left.'

Villion nodded his head. 'Then it will be your privilege to die.'

Tedric moved away from the wall before Villion had a chance to advance again. He headed for the middle of the room, covering his line of retreat with several slow, sweeping blows. Villion avoided them easily, beginning to stalk. Tedric knew he was doomed. He was losing blood – he could already see a red trail on the floor – and would not be able to stand much longer.

His head was dizzy. His vision swam. Villion had been patient with him thus far, but so close to the end he would not hesitate long before striking a final blow.

Tedric had crossed the centre of the room and was heading for the opposite wall. He started to alter his course, then made himself stop. He moved directly backward. The wall was getting close, very close. He was falling into the same trap that had nearly cost him his life a short time before. But this time he knew what he was doing. He kept his face blank as Fra Villion continued to stalk him. He flicked his wrist, making a feint. The wall couldn't be more than a metre away. Tedric took a short step back, then another one.

Now. He threw himself back and at the same time lifted his leg. Striking the wall squarely with the flat surface of his foot, he used the wall as a propulsion vehicle. Lowering his head, kicking off, he lunged forward and struck Fra Villion squarely in the chest. Caught totally by surprise, Villion had no chance to raise his whipsword. The force of impact sent both of them sprawling. Villion hit the floor on his back, and the whipsword went shooting out of his hand. Tedric clutched his weapon tightly. He rolled to his knees and he knelt above his enemy.

Among the shifting rainbow streaks of Villion's face, Tedric saw an emotion he had never guessed might reside within the Black Knight.

Fra Villion was afraid for his life.

Tedric raised his whipsword to strike a final fatal blow.

CHAPTER 13

The Revenge of Dass

Tedric waded through the steaming swamp, thick muddy water swirling around his waist. The upper part of his body, totally naked, was covered with small oozing wounds, cut by the stinging bites of the swarming insects which inhabited this desolate hell. By now, after hours of agonising progress, his nerves numbed by heat and fatigue, he barely noticed their continued presence. His blond hair lay caked close to his scalp. Sweat dripped into his eyes. He raised his left hand frequently to clear his vision, while in his right hand he gripped tightly the jewelled hilt of his longsword. The weight of that weapon, held out of the water, caused the muscles of his upper arm to ache with an extra agony.

Tedric had come to this swamp in search of a certain woman. She was the daughter of a prince and he loved her dearly.

Suddenly, he stopped. Blinking, he strained to peer through the thick mist ahead. He had seen something up there – a fleeting glimpse of ivory and ebony. It was a woman, he was sure of that.

The heavy, orange sun beat down furiously, streaking the grey mists with swirls of red, yellow, blue, and violet.

At last he saw her again. She was standing upon an islet, watching him, her legs apart, arms crossed upon bare, pale breasts.

This was not the woman he sought. That one was raven-haired and delicate. This woman was tall and strong-looking, with rich black hair and ghostly white skin.

'Hold!' he called. 'It is I, Lord Tedric of the Marshes. I must speak with you.'

A smile touched the woman's full red lips. She gestured at him. 'Come to me, Tedric.'

Then he knew her. This was the Sorceress Giana, renowned for her evil. Tedric willed his legs to cease moving as, at the same time, they plunged forward. There was no stopping his body.

The voice of Giana beat at him, a rhythmic pounding. 'Come to me,' she murmured. 'Tedric, Lord Tedric.'

He felt as if he were in a dream.

'Tedric, Tedric, Tedric.' Over and over again. 'Tedric, wake up.'

He opened his eyes.

The flat expressionless face of a Wykzl gazed down at him.

'Ky-shan,' he said.

'Tedric, you are all right?'

'I – I don't know.' He was lying on his back. With the aid of Ky-shan, he managed to reach a sitting position. There were two other men standing nearby. One looked concerned while the other seemed oblivious to all outside stimuli. Yod Cartwright and Milton Dass. He recognised them, but for the time being, the names were no more than that.

'We were afraid you'd never wake up again,' said Yod Cartwright.

Tedric gripped his head. 'I think I must have been dreaming. Where – where is this?'

'The Prison,' said Yod. 'We are Fra Villion's prisoners aboard the Iron Sphere.'

Fra Villion. The Iron Sphere. The names meant something to Tedric, started him thinking. He could remember a great deal more now. 'How long have we been here?'

'Days,' said Yod flatly. 'Villion took our timepieces but I guess we've been here four days I don't know what he intends to do with us.'

For the first time, Tedric noticed the dull pain in his right shoulder. He turned his head and saw the bandage there. The white cloth was stained red.

Yod loaned me his shirt,' Ky-shan explained. 'I did the best I could. We implored Villion to send a doctor, but he said that a true warrior must learn to endure his own wounds.'

'The code of the *vemplar*,' Tedric said bitterly.

'But you beat him,' said Yod. 'You had him down.'

Tedric shook his head. He could remember this creature Villion, remember the fight, but the details of the duel escaped him.

You could have killed him if Lola – ' Yod stopped short, glanced at the still silent Dass. 'The woman came up from behind and struck you on the head with a club.'

Tedric now noticed that his head hurt, too. He looked at the place he inhabited. It was a low-ceilinged room, with white walls, a smooth floor, and no visible doors or windows. A prison, obviously. Overhead, a single, harsh light-bulb burned. 'I shouldn't have lost,' he said.

'It was hardly your fault,' Yod said.

But Tedric knew better. He was angry at himself. He should have kept a more watchful eye and not allowed Lola Dass to work her treachery. But it was too late to worry about the past. 'If we've been here as long as you think, then the Sphere must already be on its way to Earth.'

'We entered N-space some time ago,' Ky-shan said.

'Are you sure? There's nothing to . . . '

'I can sense it. With these.' He rubbed the tips of the tendrils that sprouted from his forehead. 'It is an odd sensation, a different tone.'

'Then we may reach the Solar System at any moment.'

'I would estimate a half-dozen of your Earth days.'

'Is that another guess?' asked Yod with a grin.

'Even I require a timepiece to be absolutely certain,' replied Ky-shan.

Tedric contemplated the nearest wall. It was no different in appearance from the other three. 'Don't they feed us?' he asked.

'There's a narrow slot,' said Yod, 'and someone pushes four trays of food through every once in a while. I'm afraid we've split your share, so far. The edible portions are heavily outnumbered.'

The plastic trays were piled in a corner. The taint of rotting food reached his nostrils. Tedric counted: there were nearly thirty trays in the stack, but that meant nothing. They might be fed once, or twice or three times a day. There was no reason to expect the meals to arrive at regular intervals. 'What about the slot? Where is it?'

Yod pointed to the nearest wall. 'Somewhere in the middle of that. As soon as the trays are taken, it closes again.'

'And there's no mark in the wall?'

'None at all.'

Suddenly, Dass was screaming. It was the first sound he had made since Tedric had awakened. He stood on his spindly legs, waving both fists furiously in the air, his face flushed red with emotion. 'I'll get him!' he cried. 'I'll fix him! Trick me, will he? Play me for a fool. He'll die! All of them will die!' He spun, pointing a finger at each of them in turn. 'You will die, too.'

Tedric glanced questioningly at Yod, who merely shook his head. Dass's eyes were as wild as his words.

'He's been screaming for days,' Yod said softly, as Dass continued to rave.

'He was like this when you came?'

'Worse. To begin with he hardly shut up at all. It's all about Villion. He says he's going to kill him.'

'Does he have a way?'

Yod shrugged. 'I guess you'd have to ask him that.'

Time passed. Tedric quickly came to envy his previous unconscious state. He guessed that this cell must be located somewhere in the central core of the Sphere. It was extremely hot much of the time, and he sometimes thought he could hear the distant hum of churning machinery. He studied every nook and corner of the room. He lay on his back and peered at the ceiling, crawled on his knees and examined the floor. He watched the food when it arrived and tried to discover the location of the narrow entry slot.

But it was hopeless. He found nothing. Every passing minute drove the Iron Sphere closer to Earth, and he was trapped here. Ky-shan lapsed into silent meditation. Yod contented himself with a stream of constant chatter. Milton Dass raved and ranted. 'He stole my wife. Fra Villion, he calls himself. Well, I'll kill him. I've found a way and now he's going to pay.'

'How?' Tedric asked, more than once.

Dass stared at him blankly. Saliva dripped down his chin.

'He's as good as dead,' he insisted, with the unshakeable logic of a mad man.

The number of trays stacked in the corner reached one hundred and twenty. Some hours later the slot opened, and there were one hundred and twenty-four. Tedric reached for the food and as he did so there was the sound of an explosion.

The wall fell out.

A woman stood in the opening, with a dead man lying at her feet. She gripped a heatgun in each of her hands. She was grinning from ear-to-ear.

'You guys all right?' she asked pleasantly.

'Juvi,' shouted Yod, and rushed forward to greet her. They hugged and kissed. Yod made happy noises in the back of his throat.

The scene, complete with the charred corpse at their feet, was bizarre to say the least.

Juvi pushed Yod away and stepped into the cell. She stopped in front of Tedric, came sharply to attention, and saluted crisply.

Thoroughly confused, Tedric returned the salute.

'Allow me to introduce myself,' Juvi said. 'Lieutenant Juvi Jerome of the Imperial Corps of the One Hundred. I am here to receive your orders, sir.'

Tedric didn't know whether to be angry or amused. He compromised by grinning like an idiot. 'You could have fooled me.'

'I was supposed to, sir. Personal orders of Commander Nolan. He directed me to insinuate myself into your company and to remain anonymous for as long as possible.'

'You did a fine job of that, Juvi.'

'Thank you, sir. And now I've come to save you.'

Yod was standing off to one side, his face a mix of emotions. 'You mean you're not who you said you were?'

'My name's the same.'

'But you're not a prostitute? You're not a criminal?'

'I'm a corpsman. Or corpswoman. Take your pick.'

Tedric decided to intervene. 'Maybe we ought to take time to straighten this out later. Lieutenant Jerome, maybe you'd better fill me in on our present status. You can start by telling me how you managed to find us here. And who – ' he pointed to the corpse on the floor ' – is this?'

'Your warden, sir – the man's who's been feeding you. I knew he had to exist unless you were dead or they were starving you. It took me days to find him. When I did, I just got to know him a little better – '

Yod started to interrupt, but Tedric waved him silent.

' – and he finally brought me down here. I convinced him I was curious. I said I'd never seen a Wykzl before. Anyway, once I'd cajoled him into explaining how to open the cell, it was a simple matter to kill him and set you free.'

'And where's the present location of the Sphere?'

'That's the scary part, sir. I'm afraid we're about to enter the Solar System at any moment, if we haven't already. That's the only reason I was able to get down here. My friend – my former friend – thought he could get away with bringing me along since nearly everybody else was standing battle duty. I convinced him, even if he did get caught, I could make it worth his while.'

Yod was about to make another interruption, but a single fierce glare from Tedric was enough to quiet him this time. 'We should try to alert the imperial fleet,' Tedric said. 'Maybe we can storm the communications area and get a message through. I don't think anyone can stand against the Iron Sphere, but Earth should at least have a chance to fight.'

'Oh, I've already taken care of that, sir,' Juvi said. 'The imperial fleet ought to be ready to attack as soon as the Sphere appears.'

'But how – ?'

She grinned, as if embarrassed by her own success. 'While I was waiting to find someone who knew where you were, I made friends with a radio operator. I helped him on a couple shifts and once or twice he had to leave the room.'

Tedric shook his head, unwilling to conceal his admiration for Lieutenant Jerome's work. He was about to compliment her aloud when the floor suddenly shook.

'That must be the fleet now,' Juvi said.

Ky-shan nodded. 'I felt it a moment ago, Tedric. We are in normal space now.'

'Then we'd better hurry,' said Tedric.

'Hurry where?' asked Yod.

'Up above. There must be something we can do from the inside to help the fleet.'

'And what about him?' Yod pointed to the forlorn figure of Milton Dass. He had fallen into total silence since the arrival of Juvi, as if the rapid pace of events was too furious for him to comprehend. His eyes blinked and his mouth twitched.

'We'll bring him along. He can't very well stay down here.'

'May I offer a suggestion, sir?' said Juvi.

'Of course.'

'I think your first idea was the best one. The only way to destroy the Sphere is to destroy Fra Villion.'

'He will die!' Dass suddenly shouted. 'It is predestined!'

Juvi frowned. 'What's he talking about?'

'He's completely crazy,' said Yod.

'I wonder,' she said, gazing at Dass, who was silent once more.

Tedric returned the conversation to its original direction. 'Do you know where Villion is?'

'Not for certain, no, but if I had to make a guess, I'd look for him on the top level in the docking area. When the fleet attacks, Villion is going to have to send his ships against them. That's where I think he'll be.'

Her logic made sense. 'All right, we'll head that way.'

She saluted crisply. 'Aye, aye, sir.'

They started off, Juvi leading the way. Tedric glanced back only once, to confirm that Dass was coming, too. The inventor of the matter-scrambler trailed the pack, his eyes darting constantly as if in search of unseen pursuit.

Once they had left the twisting corridors of the inner core, progress was relatively rapid. As Juvi had predicted, there were few people about. Most could already be found in the upper levels, handling various battle duties. Fortunately, there were a few stragglers. From them, Tedric managed to obtain three additional heatguns. He gave one to Ky-shan, one to Yod, and kept the third for himself.

The Sphere continued to tremble occasionally, shaken by the impact of imperial barrages. Tedric doubted that much damage could result. The Sphere was undoubtedly well shielded. As they climbed higher, riding elevators and hauling themselves up metal-runged ladders, the shock waves abruptly ceased. After an initial surprise attack, the fleet had obviously withdrawn. Tedric knew that tactically such a manoeuvre was wise, but he still regretted the absence of the reassuring reverberations of the deck at his feet. Villion would be launching his own counter-attack now, and even if that failed, the matter-scrambler still lay readily available. Tedric felt a moment's panic, a moment's despair. If Villion hadn't used the weapon so far, it was only because he was saving it to hurl at Earth itself.

As the number of crew members around them increased, Tedric took over the lead from Juvi. He walked with brisk confidence, like a man certain of his destination. He was banking on the fact that Villion would have seen no reason to inform the majority of his forces of Tedric's attempt at assassination. They passed through a couple places plainly set up to serve as checkpoints, but none of the guards stationed at these locations did more than cursorily check their identification and wave them on. Even Dass remained cool and silent. Only the wildness of his expression revealed the true state of his mind.

The main platform in the docking area was a noisy hubbub of activity Ships were being raised from the storage hangars below for immediate transfer into open space. Tedric realised how easy it would be to board one of the ships now – the assigned crews were standing nearby, and he watched as one after another boarded the vessels that stood poised at the mouths of the dispatch tubes. But personal survival was unimportant now, for him, for all of them. Only one thing mattered – destroying Fra Villion!

Tedric spotted Bik, the watch officer he had once questioned about Fra Villion's arrival and went over to him. Tedric walked quickly, hoping to look like a man with an important message. 'Fra Villion,' he said. 'I must speak to him at once.'

Bik turned and recognised Tedric at once. He saluted. He showed no hint of surprise or suspicion, and Tedric realised he had guessed correctly about Villion's probable reticence. It made sense: no one liked to publicise the details of his own near murder. 'Villion?' said Bik. He seemed puzzled that

Tedric had even asked the question. 'Why, he's in the command centre, of course. As a matter of fact, I left his side only moments ago.' Bik's chest swelled with pride. 'He wanted my advice on the number of ships to be sent into battle at this time.'

'And I'm sure your advice was extremely helpful to Fra Villion,' Tedric said, glancing down to the access-door to the command centre.

Bik looked pleased. 'An officer of the watch should be aware of such things.'

'Of course.' Tedric moved quickly off. He waved at the others to follow. Dass was muttering softly now, but Tedric felt that any attempt to get rid of him might cause more problems than it solved. He led the way through the door. Beyond lay a narrow corridor, where a series of circular windows looked out directly on space. Tedric paused long enough to peer through one of them. That big bright yellow star there – it had to be Sol, Earth's sun. Some of the planets were undoubtedly visible, too, but he didn't have time to pick them out. Earth was still too far away. He saw a rapid-fire sequence of bright blue lights. Tractor beams, he knew, a certain sign of open space combat. Somewhere out there among the stars, a battle was raging; men were dying. He wished he could be there to take part.

The corridor turned once, then again. It widened and grew higher. There was a door ahead, with an armed man standing on each side, and Tedric recognised the entrance to the command post. He looked back and noted with satisfaction that Juvi had her hands resting lightly on her heatguns. Voices came through the door and Tedric realised that the loudest voice was that of Matthew Carey.

Stunning the guards Tedric threw open the door and stepped inside. The rhythmic hum of a computer nearly drowned out his thoughts. It was as big a machine as any he had seen outside the core of the Sphere and occupied one entire wall. There were five screens showing various views of space, a radio and speaker system, and radar equipment. There were nine figures in the room, three of whom were standing. He recognised all of them: Matthew Carey, Lola Dass, Fra Villion. Carey was the nearest to him, Villion the farthest.

None of them, as yet, were aware of his presence.

Tedric reached for his gun. It was cold-blooded, but he knew he might never get another chance. He drew the heat-gun, raised it, aimed, squeezed –

With a howl, Milton Dass slammed into his shoulder and sent the gun flying across the room.

'No!' cried Dass. 'Not now. Don't you see. He's going to die. He's doomed to die – '

The heatgun in Matthew Carey's hand erupted. The bolt caught Milton Dass squarely in the chest knocking him flat against the wall. Tedric could smell burning flesh.

Incredibly, Dass staggered forward, licking his lips, trying to speak.

Another heatgun bolt erupted from behind Tedric. It was Juvi. He saw Carey duck for cover. Fra Villion and Lola Dass were nowhere to be seen. He had failed to get off a shot, and now they had fled.

Tedric grabbed Milton Dass in his arms and drew him down to the relative safety of the floor. Dass had saved Villion's life, but for some reason Tedric was not angry. The madness had left Dass's eyes. He seemed quite sane, quite calm.

'Tell me,' said Tedric. 'Tell me what you did.'

Heatgun bolts crackled back and forth overhead, but Dass appeared not to notice. He was smiling almost beautifully. For the first time in his life – with death drawing near – the man appeared genuinely at peace. 'I fixed it,' he said, bringing his lips close to Tedric's ear so that only he could hear the words. 'As soon as I found out what they'd done to me, I took it and I fixed it. She never loved me. She went with him willingly. They made me blow up a planet, kill innocent people, and for no good reason at all.'

'No one died on Milrod Eleven,' Tedric said. 'They were all saved. I wish I could have told you before, but it was impossible.'

'Saved? By whom?'

'The Scientists.'

'You wouldn't lie to me, Tedric?'

'Not about that.'

Dass closed his eyes. 'Thank God for that.' Tedric wished he could let him die in peace, but there was one more thing he had to know.

'You said you fixed it. What was it you fixed, Milton? How is it going to happen?'

His eyes fluttered open. 'You mean you haven't guessed? The matter-scrambler, of course. When Fra Villion turns it on, when he's ready to blow up Earth and kill billions, *blooey*, it's going to backfire right in his face. I reversed certain controls. It'll destroy the Iron Sphere, and itself as well.'

'And Fra Villion.'

Dass tried to smile, but his face twisted with pain. 'Especially Fra Villion,' he managed to gasp.

'Then why didn't you let me kill him before? When I had the chance?'

'Because I wanted to do it, not you. I was the one who hated him.'

Tedric felt a tugging at his sleeve. He glanced up and saw Ky-shan crouching beside him. 'We have to hurry, Tedric. We have to escape.'

Tedric nodded and looked back at Dass. His eyes were shut now, and his chest was motionless. 'Ky-shan, give me your heatgun,' Tedric said.

The Wykzl complied unhesitantly.

Tedric rose to his feet and, ignoring the scattering of fire around him, turned the heatgun on the radio console. He fired several bolts into the rig, then turned and darted towards the door. Yod and Juvi were waiting for him there.

'We missed Villion,' she said bitterly.

'Maybe,' said Tedric. 'Is the corridor clear? If it is, I want you two and Ky-shan to make a break while I cover you. Head for the docking area. It's our only chance.'

'But Villion – ' Yod began.

'But nothing,' said Tedric. He gave the youngster a shove. 'The three of you get out of here.'

Carey and the others continued to fire randomly, their aim poor, as the mass of equipment in the room prevented them from sighting in on their intended targets. Tedric hurled his fire more strategically. He aimed a bolt at the computer console, then fired a blast at the radar screen. He placed two over the top of Carey's head, then finished off the radio; firing a final burst in Carey's direction, he then sprang for the door. Juvi, fortunately, had left it open and he slid through the gap on his belly and rolled to his feet in the corridor.

The three of them were waiting for him. 'Get out of here!' he yelled impatiently. 'I'll catch up with you. Head for the docks.'

Stepping forward, he slid the door shut. Then, standing poised, he let his heatgun wash across the face of the door, melting the hard plastic surface and sealing it closed. Carey would be able to burn himself free in time, but he could not be sure that Tedric wasn't waiting in the corridor for him to emerge. With the radio console out of commission, an alarm could not be raised. All Tedric wanted was time to reach the docks, grab one of the waiting ships, and soar to freedom. Of course, there was Fra Villion. He had fled, but to where? It was likely that Villion had alerted his men to the danger of internal sabotage.

With the door safely sealed, Tedric turned and raced down the corridor. It remained deserted. At one point, he passed a man heading in the opposite direction, but received hardly a questioning glance. That was one good thing about combat conditions. A man in a hurry aroused no especial interest.

Tedric caught up with Ky-shan and the others at the door that led into the docks. The four of them paused there, gathering up their collective energy.

'What now, sir?' Juvi asked.

'Only one thing we can do,' Tedric said. 'Wait until a ship has been raised to the tubes, then hop aboard. It's a computer process to launch one and I doubt they'll have time to stop us.'

'Won't they be expecting us?'

'I burned out the radio.'

'Will Villion be there?'

'I have no way of knowing.'

'I'd like to get another shot at him – without Dass.'

Tedric shook his head. 'Don't bother. The main thing now is for us to get out of here.'

'Why?'

'Something Dass told me. I'll explain later. Let's go.'

They went through the door and hurried down the platform. Tedric motioned them over to the place where the various crews were waiting to board. He glanced across the platform, spotting Bik, who was staring back at him curiously. Tedric smiled and stuck a thumb up. Bik waved back and looked away, satisfied for the moment. Tedric thought that a moment would be quite long enough.

A ship was rising already. In another minute it would be poised at the mouth of the tube, ready to receive its crew. Tedric edged forward and let his hand drop to his waist.

Yod tugged his sleeve. 'Look there,' he said. 'It's him.'

Tedric turned his head. Fra Villion stood on the platform in plain view. He was looking right at Tedric.

'I could try to get off a shot,' Juvi said tentatively.

'No,' said Tedric.

'But we can't just let him escape,' Yod cried angrily.

'Do as I say,' Tedric snapped. He laid a hand on Yod's shoulder. 'It's taken care of – I promise you.'

'Villion would never expose himself like that unless he knew he could get away,' Juvi said bitterly.

'But why is he just standing there?' said Yod. 'He can see us. Why doesn't he do something?'

Tedric wasn't prepared to answer that. Villion's gaze never wavered for an instant, but around him, work continued as before.

Tedric turned his head back. The ship had arrived. Three men broke away from the waiting group and headed for the open lock. Tedric stepped in front of them and levelled his heatgun.

'Stay where you are. I'm taking this ship. The next one will be yours.'

The men swivelled their heads, wide-eyed, but when they saw Fra Villion watching them in apparent contentment, they relaxed.

'Back off,' said Tedric. He motioned Yod, Juvi, and Kyshan past him towards the ship. He was watching Fra Villion, too. Suddenly Villion raised one big hairy hand and placed it across his forehead. As impossible as it seemed, Tedric could swear he was smiling.

And he's saluting me, he thought. He's telling me good-bye. He really doesn't know!

Only Yod hesitated at the lock, and then he, too, disappeared inside. Tedric waited another moment torn by indecision; it would have been so easy to shoot Fra Villion, to make absolutely sure . . . A figure materialised beside the Bioman. It was Lola Dass. Villion took her bare arm in one hand and stroked it tenderly.

Abruptly, Tedric turned and headed for the ship. He jumped through the open lock and told Juvi to seal the gap. Yod Cartwright was watching him in total bewilderment, and with not a little anger; he still failed to understand what was happening.

The ship was already gliding down the smooth plastic interior of the tube on its way to the open gate that led to outer space.

'Take the back controls,' he told Ky-shan. 'I'll fly her. Juvi, can you work the radio?'

'I can try.'

'Once we're in space, contact the fleet. Try the regular frequencies and hope they're using one of them. Ask for Phillip Nolan. Tell them you're calling for Tedric and that it's urgent. When you get him, let me know.'

'Aye, aye, sir.'

Tedric adjusted the ship's viewscreens. Ahead, he could see the growing circle of darkness that represented the freedom of space. Suddenly, it was all round them. 'We're out,' he said softly.

'And he never tried to stop us.' Yod stood at Tedric's shoulder. 'Why did he do that? He could have had us killed at any moment.'

Tedric set the forward viewscreen to show the area ahead where the flashes of blue light indicated the battle was raging. He turned the rear screen to reflect the dwindling bulk of the Iron Sphere. 'There was no way he could have killed me,' he said irritably. 'Are you so stupid you can't see that?'

'I don't understand –'

'Fra Villion is a *vemplar*, a knight. They possess a rigid code of behaviour. I defeated him in an honest duel. He should have died. After that, there was no way he could kill me.' Tedric glanced coldly at the boy. 'As for you, you're just damned lucky.'

'But he was holding us prisoner.'

'Until after the battle, yes. If he had succeeded, he would have let us go then. Fortunately, Juvi prevented us from having to wait for that.'

'But he's still going to win. There's nothing that can stop him.'

'We'll have to see about that,' Tedric said. He stared down at the screen, watching the Iron Sphere as it floated in the void; and as he watched so the outline of a ship appeared dimly, soaring past the Sphere's edge. Tedric felt his mouth go dry.

'I've got him, sir,' Juvi called from the back of the cockpit. 'It's Commander Nolan.'

'Keep your eyes on the screens and tell me if there's any major change,' Tedric told Yod. Then he hurried back to the radio console. The familiar features of his old friend Phillip Nolan showed on the tiny screen.

'We've got them on the run,' Nolan's slightly distorted voice said from the radio receiver. 'We've got one ship to their ten. Hurry up and get here, Tedric, and join the fun.'

'I'm coming, but there's something you have to do first. Withdraw the fleet. Get all your ships back to Earth as quickly as you can.'

'But –'

Tedric hated to waste time explaining. Every second that passed meant the possibility of unnecessary slaughter. Villion was beaten, and there was no reason to fight. 'I know what I'm saying, Phillip. Those ships are just a diversion. The Iron Sphere itself is –'

The radio flew away from him. Tedric was hurled high into the air and sent crashing to the deck by the artificial gravity of the spinning ship. Yod was shouting. Juvi was screaming. Tedric landed painfully, his head spinning, but he knew he had to see.

Staggering to his feet, he stumbled towards the pilot's console. Yod had also been knocked to the floor. There was blood on his forehead, but his eyes were open.

Tedric looked at the rear viewscreens. He blinked and shook his head to be sure what he was seeing was really there.

He saw nothing.

Where the Iron Sphere had once floated, now there was only emptiness.

CHAPTER 14

Into the Red Cloud

Slumped deep in his chair, painfully aware of the immense fatigue that numbed his body, Tedric raised the mug to his lips and sipped tentatively, letting the steaming brew wash across his lips and tongue before he finally swallowed. He felt an immediate burst of renewed energy; the drink acted on him like a night's restful sleep.

'What is it?' he asked Phillip Nolan, Commander of the Imperial Corps of the One Hundred, who sat across from him.

'A hot green *cesma*,' said Nolan. 'It's an alien concoction from the region of Sirius. A favourite among pirates, I understand. I thought you might have acquired a taste.'

Tedric took another swallow. 'I hadn't, but I may. This is superb.'

Nolan smiled wanly. The two of them were seated in his cabin aboard the imperial battlecruiser, *Eagleseye*, which had served as Admiral Mallard's flagship during the recent battle with the Iron Sphere.

After a moment of thoughtful silence, Nolan said, 'Why did you let him escape?'

Tedric lowered his mug and stared into the distance. 'I don't know, Phillip. I just don't know. I saw the ship slip away just a few moments before the explosion – it was unquestionably Villion –'

'A feeling? A Tedric intuition?'

'What else?' Tedric smiled as he watched his friend. 'Will action be taken against me?'

'Should it be?'

'I let a known criminal escape. That could be interpreted as cowardice.'

Nolan shrugged his braided shoulders. 'What court in the Empire could make a charge of cowardice stick against you, Tedric – unless it was by mutual agreement.' Both men laughed. After a moment, Nolan said, more seriously, 'Where do you think he would go?'

'Back to the red cloud, I would imagine.'

'Why?'

'I can't be sure, but I think he uses it as a gateway. If he entered the Empire that way, he may be leaving by the same route.'

'And you think the woman's with him, too.'

Again, it's just a feeling, but I doubt that he'd ever leave her willingly. 'Have you seen Lola Dass?'

'Only as a child. We went to school together. She was beautiful then.'

'And she still is.'

'But Villion is gone. Isn't that the real point? We'll never see him again.'

Tedric shook his head. 'I wish I were sure.'

'Another feeling?'

'Almost.'

'Well, there are a lot of things I'm not sure about,' Nolan said. 'For instance, if Villion knew the Sphere was going to be destroyed, why didn't he just stop and repair the damage to the matter-scrambler?'

'I doubt that he could have. Dass was a genius. Only he knew enough to fix what he had done, and he was dead.'

'But why did the Sphere explode when it did? I thought Villion intended to attack Earth.'

'I'm only guessing. When he left, I think Villion gave the order to fire the gun that contained the matter-scrambler.'

'To shield his own escape?'

'Yes, partly. And to make sure the Sphere didn't fall into our hands.'

'That would have been a prize.' Nolan sipped his own drink, a more conventional beer. 'At least Matthew Carey's dead.'

'Probably, but who knows? Maybe Villion took him along, too.'

'I should have suspected something when he disappeared from Earth. It happened just after the destruction of Milrod Eleven. I should have made some connection.'

'How could you have guessed? Villion had apparently been counselling Carey for some time by image projection. Carey hinted that much to me. There was no way for you to know.'

'I suppose not. Still, I'm just glad it's over. There's nothing else we can do.'

'Isn't there?' Finishing his drink, Tedric edged forward. 'That's something I've been wanting to ask you about. I think someone ought to go after Fra Villion.'

'You mean follow him into the red cloud?'

'Yes.'

'Who do you have in mind?' Nolan grinned crookedly. 'Not yourself, maybe?'

'I've come this far. I can't say I know Villion better than anyone else, but I sense that he is frightened of me. That's a powerful weapon against one such as he.'

Nolan was shaking his head. 'I still don't think I can authorise it. The Wykzl regard the clouds as killers. I won't send you off on a suicide mission.'

'I'm willing to take the risk.'

Nolan lowered his head. 'I'll have to consider it.'

Tedric knew, as far as Phillip was concerned, that was nearly as good as a *yes*.

There was a knock on the door. Nolan jumped to his feet expectantly and hurried to the door. He opened it, hesitated for a moment, slipped through the gap, and disappeared.

Puzzled, Tedric rose and walked across the room. He stopped, heart racing, as Lady Alyc Carey stepped into the room and walked across to him.

'Then you are all right,' he said, as if this hadn't been the very first thing he'd ascertained upon reaching the *Eagleseye*.

She extended her hands, and Tedric caught them. 'You saved my life,' she said.

'No, not me. It was Skandos, the Scientist. He came to me and promised you wouldn't be hurt. I was the one who destroyed Milrod Eleven. It was your home. I'm sorry for that.'

'No, it's better,' she said quickly. 'I had too many ugly memories there. Phillip found me a home on Earth. I feel freer now than ever before.'

'Did Skandos send you directly to Earth? I never knew.'

'He did. To the imperial palace. Right outside Phillip's room. I told him what had happened to me. He must have thought I was crazy. Then he found out about Milrod Eleven and he wasn't so sure.'

'And Kisha and Kuevee?'

'They're with me. They were brought to Earth, too. Not the palace, but I found them.'

'I'm just glad no one was harmed.'

'I have a garden here, too. Won't you come see it?'

'I – ' He paused, not sure what to say. 'I may not be able . . . ' He stopped.

She was laughing.

He took her in his arms. Their lips met at last. The kiss was a long one. Finally, as Alyc drew away. 'My voices told me about you. They said you were going on a very long journey.'

He grinned. 'You sound like a fortune-teller.'

'No, but I know you. What is it this time? More pirates?'

He told her about Villion's escape and about the red cloud.

'You could be killed,' she said.

'Possibly.'

'Then you won't come to my new home and stay with me forever?'

The offer was tempting. 'I wish I could.' And he knew that was true, as true as the fact that he was inherently incapable of saying yes.

'But you don't intend to leave immediately?'

'I suppose not.'

'Then, when we get back to Earth, come and stay with me. Make it a day, a week, a month, however long you want. We don't have to set an ending. Will you do that for me?'

'For us both,' he said.

She took his hand. In spite of her blindness, she moved through the room like a wraith. He followed, guessing her intended destination. They went into a second room and stayed there.

CHILDREN'S BOOKS

SCIENCE FICTION

0426200500	Terrance Dicks **STAR QUEST: SPACEJACK**	60p
0426200160	A. M. Lightner **STAR DOG**	60p*

ADOLESCENT NON-FICTION
(also listed under Star General Non-Fiction)

Star

0352302690	Lynne Reid Banks **MY DARLING VILLIAN**	70p
0352302712	Judy Blume **FOREVER**	60p
0352303271	Alan Parker **PUDDLES IN THE LANE**	75p

ADOLESCENT FICTION
(also listed under Star General Fiction

0352304790	Judith Midgley-Carver and Amanda Duckett **CAREER CHOICES** **A Guide to Making the Right Decision (Illus)**	70p
0352302704	Peter Mayle **WILL I LIKE IT? (Colour Illus)**	£1.95*

†For sale in Britain and Ireland only.
*Not for sale in Canada. •Reissues.
♦ Film & T.V. tie-ins.

	ISBN	Author / Title	Price
Δ	0426118936	Philip Hinchcliffe DOCTOR WHO AND THE MASQUE OF MANDRAGORA	70p
Δ	0426112520	Terrance Dicks DOCTOR WHO AND THE PLANET OF THE DALEKS	60p
Δ	0426106555	Terrance Dicks DOCTOR WHO AND THE PLANET OF THE SPIDERS	70p
Δ	0426200616	Terrance Dicks DOCTOR WHO AND THE ROBOTS OF DEATH	70p
Δ	042611308X	Malcolm Hulke DOCTOR WHO AND THE SEA-DEVILS	70p
Δ	0426116585	Philip Hinchcliffe DOCTOR WHO AND THE SEEDS OF DOOM	60p
Δ	0426200497	Ian Marter DOCTOR WHO AND THE SONTARAN EXPERIMENT	60p
Δ	0426110331	Malcolm Hulke DOCTOR WHO AND THE SPACE WAR	60p
Δ	0426119738	Terrance Dicks DOCTOR WHO AND THE TALONS OF WENG-CHIANG	60p
Δ	0426115007	Terrance Dicks DOCTOR WHO AND THE TERROR OF THE AUTONS	60p
Δ	0426200233	Terrance Dicks DOCTOR WHO AND THE TIME WARRIOR	60p
Δ	0426113241	Bill Strutton DOCTOR WHO AND THE ZARBI (illus)	70p
Δ	0426200012	Terrance Dicks THE SECOND DOCTOR WHO MONSTER BOOK (Colour illus)	70p
	0426118421	Terrance Dicks DOCTOR WHO DINOSAUR BOOK	75p
	0426116151	Terrance Dicks and Malcolm Hulke THE MAKING OF DOCTOR WHO	60p
	0426200020	DOCTOR WHO DISCOVERS PREHISTORIC ANIMALS (NF) (illus)	75p

†For sale in Britain and Ireland only.
*Not for sale in Canada.
♦ Film & T.V. tie-ins.

Δ	0426112792	Terrance Dicks **DOCTOR WHO AND THE GIANT ROBOT**	70p
Δ	0426115430	Malcolm Hulke **DOCTOR WHO AND THE GREEN DEATH**	60p
Δ	0426200330	Terrance Dicks **DOCTOR WHO AND THE HAND OF FEAR**	60p
Δ	0426200098	Terrance Dicks **DOCTOR WHO AND THE HORROR OF FANG ROCK**	70p
Δ	0426200772	Terrance Dicks **DOCTOR WHO AND THE IMAGE OF THE FENDAHL**	70p
Δ	0426200543	Terrance Dicks **DOCTOR WHO AND THE INVISIBLE ENEMY**	60p
	0426200039	**DOCTOR WHO DISCOVERS SPACE TRAVEL (NF) (illus)**	75p
	0426200047	**DOCTOR WHO DISCOVERS STRANGE AND MYSTERIOUS CREATURES (NF) (illus)**	75p
	042620008X	**DOCTOR WHO DISCOVERS THE STORY OF EARLY MAN (NF) (illus)**	75p
	0426200136	**DOCTOR WHO DISCOVERS THE CONQUERORS (NF) (illus)**	75p

† For sale in Britain and Ireland only.
* Not for sale in Canada.
♦ Film & T.V. tie-ins.

Wyndham Books are obtainable from many booksellers and newsagents. If you have any difficulty please send purchase price plus postage on the scale below to:

Wyndham Cash Sales:
P O Box 11,
Falmouth,
Cornwall.

or

Star Book Service:
G P O Box 29,
Douglas,
Isle of Man,
British Isles.

While every effort is made to keep prices low, it is sometimes necessary to increase prices at short notice. Wyndham Books reserve the right to show new retail prices on covers which may differ from those advertised in the text or elsewhere.

Postage and Packing Rate
UK
22p for the first book plus 10p per copy for each additional book ordered to a maximum charge of 82p.

BFPO and Eire
22p for the first book, plus 10p per copy for the next 6 books and thereafter 4p per book.

Overseas
30p for the first book and 10p per copy for each additional book.

These charges are subject to Post Office charge fluctuations.